unbreak me

unbreak me

by LEXI RYAN

This book is a work of fiction. Any resemblance to institutions or persons, living or dead, is purely coincidental.

Copyediting by Editing720
Cover © 2013 Sarah Hansen, Okay Creations
Interior formatting by E.M. Tippetts Book Designs

dedication

To Jack and Mary

about this book

Unbreak Me is New Adult contemporary romance. Due to sexual content and heavy subject matter, it is intended for mature readers.

"If you're broken, I'll fix you…"

I'm only twenty-one and already damaged goods. A slut. A failure. A disappointment to my picture-perfect family as long as I can remember. I called off my wedding to William Bailey, the only man who thought I was worth fixing. A year later and he's marrying my sister.

Unless I ask him not to…

"If you shatter, I'll find you…"

But now there's Asher Logan, a broken man who sees the fractures in my façade and doesn't want to fix me at all. Asher wants me to stop hiding, to stop pretending. Asher wants to break down my walls. But that means letting him see my ugly secrets and forgiving him for his.

With my past weighing down on me, do I want the man who holds me together or the man who gives me permission to break?

chapter one

Maggie

"YOU'RE NOT going to flake out, are you?"

I blink before realizing what my sister means. It's time. Time for me to face this. Time for me to pretend *everything is just fine.*

Time for me to walk down the aisle.

The words swim in my head. *Walk. Down. Aisle.* As if it's no big deal. As if I'm okay with this.

Lizzy gives me a shove toward the doors.

I can hear it now. The organ. Processional music. The hum of the crowd's whispers.

"Put a smile on your face and *march*," Krystal hisses.

I show her my middle finger before pushing through the doors.

"It's going to be okay," I hear Lizzy say. "She's going to do it."

My sisters' murmurs fade as I focus on my task.

My stomach pitches and my hands shake behind my bouquet, but I plaster on a smile and time my steps to the organ's heavy chords.

That's when I see him.

William Bailey stands at the front of the church, hands clasped in front of him. His eyes are hot and desperate and all over me. Can the guests see it too? The longing that rolls off him in waves as I approach?

Is he thinking the same thing I am? That this is supposed to be us? That this is supposed to be *our* wedding?

Or is he thinking I was the biggest mistake of his life?

I can't go there. Not here. Not now. I pretend not to notice the questions in his eyes, pretend not to notice the hum of gossip swelling around me.

But underneath the taffeta and flowers, underneath the hoopskirt and pretense, I'm overwhelmed with the thought that *this* is what my life has come to. Just a bridesmaid. Just a bridesmaid in my sister's wedding.

Just a bridesmaid in my sister's wedding to my ex-fiancé.

A vocalist joins the organ and the hum of whispers quiets—a swarm of killer bees distracted from their target as they remember the reason for their presence.

I reach the end of the aisle, ankles and dignity still intact, and breathe a sigh of relief as the congregation turns their attention to the next bridesmaid.

My sisters march one by one, coordinating with the hydrangea-blue décor like giant chameleons.

The flower girl appears at the end of the aisle, and the crowd stands.

Something in my chest tugs long and hard at the sight of my youngest sister. Even at ten years old, she's a delicate little thing with a tiny voice and a big brain. Too young to be a bridesmaid but too old to be a flower girl, she looks like a child bride half-drowned in white tulle.

Finally, Krystal enters. Thick brown curls piled high on her head and a smile curving her lips, she embodies every little girl's wedding-day dream.

Cameras flash. Women sigh. Tissues abound.

My eyes slide to Will again, and I'm not surprised to see he's watching me. For the hundredth time since I returned home last month, I find myself remembering the comfort of his arms. Why couldn't I have stayed there?

As his bride reaches center aisle, Will takes a step toward her.

He's going through with this. He's really going to marry her.

The same moment he takes her hand, the air conditioning kicks on.

First there are murmurs, whispers that carry back through the congregation and have me and my sisters exchanging confused glances.

Will shuffles back, scrambling to cover his mouth.

My mom's eyes roll back in her head, and she falls to the floor.

A breath later, I smell it. The scent guarantees Krystal's wedding will be as unforgettable as she dreamed.

No one would forget the wedding that smelled of rotting carcass.

A gag settles at the back of my throat as the smell grows.

My sisters hide their noses in their bouquets.

Seconds later, the bride gasps. Her face crumbles and she *howls*.

The sounds of retching echo through the church as the guests run toward the exits, pushing and shoving their way to fresh air.

The priest looks lost, and I nail him with my gaze. *Do something, damn it!* And he does.

He gags right into his microphone.

Chaos breaks loose. More gagging. Scrambling. Pushing.

No one cares about the wedding anymore. No one cares about vows or five-thousand-dollar dresses—not in the middle of stench warfare.

My little sister's face is white with panic. Her jaw slack as the chaos grows.

I offer my hand. "Come on."

She stares at me, then opens her mouth and throws up all over her dress, her face crumbling in horror.

Poor thing.

Grabbing her hand, I urge her toward the exit. "Abby!" When she doesn't move, I gather her lanky frame into my arms and sweep her out of the church.

We make it out the doors and to the sidewalk where Krystal is crying into Will's arms. He strokes her hair, helpless, and whispers something in her ear.

When he lifts his head, the evening sunlight frames his messy blond hair and our eyes lock. It feels like we have a lifetime between us. A lifetime since my lies fooled us both. A lifetime since I believed a girl like me could have a happily-ever-after.

The reception tent glows with candlelight, and the soft May breeze

3

floats up from the river, jingling the wind chimes. Krystal and Will's reception is set up on the vast green expanse of my mother's backyard, just like mine was supposed to be last year.

Just like *ours* was supposed to be.

They're words I can't dwell on, but avoiding them leaves my mind hopping from place to place like a panicked rabbit in a den of wolves.

Topiaries line the path down the hill and to the river, and I follow them, needing to see the rushing water and escape the music and laughter and joviality. I can feel Will's eyes on me as I slip from the tent, but I don't go to him.

Krystal begged me to come home for the wedding, to be her bridesmaid so everyone would know things were okay between us, so everyone would know I was okay with her marrying my ex. I had my own reasons for doing it, but I can't talk to Will.

Not yet. Not here.

I can't stop thinking about what happened at the chapel. My mother and the wedding planner awkwardly organized the guests and directed them to the reception, where dinner was served. Now dancing is in full swing. But what about the ceremony? Does this mean Krystal and Will aren't married? They never said vows. Did they find some dark corner to sign the papers?

Of course, I can't ask. Everyone will think it's because I want Will for myself. They'll think I'm asking because I'm not over him.

I'm halfway down the path when I spot a man a few yards beyond my mother's dock. His black dress pants and a dress shirt draw my attention to the wide expanse of his shoulders and the narrow taper of his hips. I don't know him, but I recognize a kindred spirit. He looks hurt and far away, hands tucked into his pockets, gaze locked on the water. A broken heart left behind when Krystal put Will's ring on her finger?

I hesitate for a minute. I was looking for some solitude down here, but I'm drawn to this man who looks as lost and lonely as I feel.

I hop off the paved path, and my heels sink into the soft earth as I approach him.

"You look a little lost," I say. When he turns to me, his eyes are weary. I recognize that too and stall mid-step. "I don't think we've met. I'm Maggie Thompson, sister of the bride."

"I'm Asher."

Asher. Asher. I scan my memory for the significance of the name but I can't find it. New Hope is a small town, and I don't recognize him, but that doesn't mean much since my mom invited half the state of Indiana and a good portion of Kentucky. "Asher what? Friend of the bride or groom?"

"Just Asher. And I'm not a wedding guest."

Oh. That explains it. "Just one name? Like Madonna?"

His lips quirk. "Something like that."

"Nice to meet you, Just Asher." I offer my hand, and when he takes it, I can't help but notice the size and heat of his. An image flashes through my mind—rough fingers skimming over my bare skin, those eyes sweeping over my exposed body.

Asher should be the poster child for the sexy bad boy. I bet he even has a few tats under that pressed dress shirt. He's a big guy, not just tall but large, solid, filling his black oxford in a way that makes it difficult to keep from staring.

Hell, staring is inevitable. Not *drooling* is difficult.

His dark, messy hair has a little curl to it, the kind of hair a woman can slide between her fingers while her lover explores her body.

His stubbled cheeks inspire some inappropriate fantasies, and that cocky grin says he knows just what I'm thinking.

"Maggie?"

The little voice stops my thoughts and my heart, and I turn to see my youngest sister.

Abby changed clothes after the would-be ceremony and now wears a little pink dress. Just looking at her makes my heart ache. She grew up so much while I was away, and knowing how much I missed gnaws at me. I wasn't around to protect her from our mother's unachievable standards. Abby may be the one person in this world who really needs me.

"Hey, sweetie," I say.

"Hey, Mags." She toys with the hem of her dress. "I'm sorry about what happened at the church. I freaked out."

Something unwelcome sticks at the back of my throat at that insecurity in her eyes, that need to be everything to everyone at only ten years old. "It's okay. We all panicked a little."

"I missed you," she whispers.

Even though I've been home nearly four weeks, I've been making myself scarce, and this is the first she's mentioned my absence. The words claw at my heart and I pull her into a hug. She wraps her arms around my neck and I inhale deeply.

"Are you mad I got upchuck on your pretty dress?"

I flash a grin back to the sexy stranger and shake my head. "I don't know what pretty dress you're talking about. I've been wearing this ugly thing all day."

Abby stifles a giggle behind her hand.

"Abby," someone calls.

William.

He's headed down the hill toward us. "Your sister needs you for a few more pictures," he tells her.

"But I don't want to take more pictures," Abby whispers, a rare complaint from a people-pleasing child.

"Go on now. It's important to Krystal."

Abby nods. "Bye, Maggie," she says as she scurries away.

Will watches her go. When he turns to me, his expression shifts from stoic to pained.

"Are you married? Is it official?" How ironic that he's the only one here I trust enough to ask.

"No." The word is so soft I almost miss it.

"So…now what?"

His eyes devour me. It's been a year since I was his, and it's like he's trying to catalogue every new freckle, trying to account for every missed smile. "We haven't decided yet."

I open my mouth to speak then close it. My throat is so tight there's no room for words. I can't identify the emotion strangling me. Hope that he'll give me another chance? Fear that he might?

"Maggie." He breathes my name like a prayer, but then says, "It doesn't change anything. We're getting married. I love her. She wants to make a life with me."

I force a smile to hide that he's just smacked me with his words. Krystal wants to make a life with him, and I hadn't.

Not true, my mind objects. But I know that's what he must think. It's what I'd made him think.

Will notices the stranger for the first time. I'd forgotten about him, but he's still there, watching us carefully. "What's he doing here?"

"He's with me," I blurt. "Krystal said I could bring a date." The impulse to make Will think I'm attached is kneejerk, but I regret my words as soon as I see the man's eyebrows lift. I didn't mean for him to hear me, and horror sweeps over my face in hot waves.

But instead of calling me on my lie, Asher comes to my side and wraps his arm loosely around my shoulders. "I didn't want my girl to have to dance alone."

Will blinks then jerks back, and, as if we're tied together by invisible threads, I have to fight the instinct to follow.

"The bar opens in ten," he says. "Enjoy yourselves." With that, he turns and heads back to the reception.

When he's gone, I step out of the stranger's embrace. "You didn't want your girl to dance alone?"

"You started it." He grins full-out now, and my heart damn near stops in my chest. Sexy Stranger goes from hot to *panty-melting* when he grins.

"Are you prepared to continue this charade all night?" I ask. "To dance and pretend you like a total stranger just to help her out of an awkward conversation?"

He shrugs. "I can think of worse ways to spend my time." He slides his gaze over me. When he returns to my face, I notice his eyes for the first time. Wolf eyes. A blue so icy it's nearly colorless, rimmed by a dark ring.

This might not be the worst day of my life after all.

"Want to check out that open bar?" I ask, nodding toward the reception. "My family is loaded, so I'm sure it's stocked with the good stuff." I'm already heading in that direction, hoping he'll follow, hoping the company of a stranger will keep people and all their polite inquiries far away.

"Do you dance?" Asher stops me before I can make it to the bar.

"Not even a little."

He has Bad Boy written all over him, and my mom is going to flip when she sees me on his arm. Of course, this only enhances the appeal.

"Okay. I give up," Asher says. "I can't figure it out." His eyes connect with mine and send a little buzz through me.

I thought I'd lost that—the ability to get a buzz from the way a boy looks at me.

This is no boy, my mind tells me. *This is a man.* I'm no stranger to older men, but when I came back to New Hope, it was with a promise to myself that things would be different. That *I'd* be different. And yet here I am, preparing to spend my evening with a sexy stranger who breaks all the New Me rules.

"What's making you crazy?"

"I know you from somewhere…"

I have to laugh at that. "That line? Really? If you're trying to pick me up, can't you at least amuse me by coming up with something unique?"

He flashes that wicked, devil-may-care grin again and my goddamn stomach does a little flip. "Is that what you think I'm trying to do?"

I shrug. "I don't really know. It's been a long time since I bothered with games."

He steps closer, looking down at me. "Because you get right to the point?"

He guides me to the dance floor, and I let him.

Etta James croons from the speakers as this beautiful bad boy pulls me into his arms, his eyes roaming over my face like this is foreplay. He's a man who makes dancing easy, guiding me around so smoothly I could be walking on clouds.

When he dips his head, his mouth brushes my ear. "You know, don't you, that by dancing with me, you're going to make people whisper about you all night?"

I squeeze my eyes shut for a moment. They are whispering about me, it's true, but the whispers have nothing to do with some mystery man.

It was a year ago, but my wedding to William Bailey is still the hottest kind of gossip. A wedding called off two days before the bride and groom were scheduled to say their vows? Young bride ran away to God-knows-where for an entire year? Hell, the people of New Hope usually have to steal the mayor's cable to get stories that juicy.

"It doesn't matter," I murmur. Over Asher's shoulder, my three older sisters watch me with unhinged jaws. What's with them?

The song ends and the crowd on the dance floor shifts. Some couples return to their seats and others slide into each other's arms.

Asher grins. "I thought you didn't dance?"

"I don't. Couldn't you tell?" I shiver under his hot gaze. One dance and I'm contemplating bridesmaid clichés and one-night stands.

The DJ transitions to another song, and I find myself moving into his arms again. We fall into the rhythm of the music, and I'm rethinking my aversion to dancing when I feel a vibration from his hip. He's busy tracing my shoulder with the rough pad of his thumb and doesn't notice.

"Is that a cell phone in your pocket," I whisper up at him, "or did I misplace my vibrator?"

He pulls away and reaches for his phone. "You're something else." He glances at the number on the display. "I have to take this. It was nice to meet you, Maggie. Thank you for the dance." He winks at me as he backs away, leaving me grinning on the edge of the dance floor, dumb with lust.

My good mood vanishes when I turn and see Will and Krystal dancing.

My Will, I catch myself thinking. Which isn't fair, and I know that, but I keep remembering his arms wrapped around me and his breath in my hair as he whispered, *"If you're broken, I'll fix you."*

His thumb brushes her cheek, and he's looking at her with such tenderness, I stumble over my own feet in my rush to get off the dance floor. Loneliness claws at me, digging into my flesh just deeply enough that my eyes wet with tears.

chapter two

William

I AM an addict.

I am the cocky asshole who thinks he's bigger than his addiction. I am the ignorant son of a bitch who thinks he can look temptation in the face and walk away.

I have never been so wrong about anything.

Like most addicts, I can't tell you when my addiction began. I can't tell you the moment when my fondness for her became something more compelling. More dangerous. Was it when she was fifteen and showed up in my dorm room at Notre Dame? The girl next door suddenly a curvy vixen with sad eyes and hungry hands? Was it when I came back home for graduate school and she became a constant in my life? Or did it only begin when I tasted her lips for the first time, the sun reflecting off the water, the breeze ruffling our hair?

Maybe addictions don't have a beginning. They certainly don't have an end.

The bathroom door jars open and I remember myself. Who I am. Where I am.

She's staring at me, arms wrapped around herself as if her long, hot shower left her cold. "You could feign a little disappointment, you know."

Krystal is pissed. Hell, she should be. Today was everything to her. She'd planned every detail, as if the perfect wedding might make the guests forget I was supposed to marry her sister first. But it was ruined. And no one forgets.

"I am disappointed," I protest. Even to my own ears I sound apathetic, but I'm not, dammit, I'm just…weak.

"You need to tell me the truth." She settles on the bed, the hotel's fluffy white robe enveloping her petite frame. "Are you relieved? Do you feel like you dodged a bullet?" Her voice wavers, as if she's struggling to hold back tears, and I feel like the world's biggest asshole.

"No." I take her hands in mine. Squeeze her fingertips against my palms. "I want to marry you."

Her big brown eyes search my face, reading it for signs of a relapse. "You haven't been the same since she's been home."

There's no correct way I can respond to this and we both know it. Agreement will only prime her insecurities. Disagreement would be the lie that will drive this growing wedge between us. "I want to marry you," I repeat. "Let's do it again. A new ceremony. A new reception. Whatever you want."

She blinks at me and forces a smile. "Okay."

"I love you." I sound a little desperate. Maybe I am.

She leans her head against my shoulder, and her wet hair seeps through my shirt and chills my skin. One month ago, this bond between us was enough. One month ago, when I told Krystal I loved her, I didn't have a devil on my shoulder weighing that love against my love for someone else. One month ago, Maggie was out of my system.

I close my eyes with every intention to focus on Krystal, on my love for her, hers for me. Our future. Instead, I see Maggie lying by the river after a heavy rain, her hair splayed in a red sunburst against the lush green grass as she listens to the rushing water. I see Maggie's sprinkle of freckles and Maggie's bright green eyes laughing at me.

Krystal sniffs into my chest and I draw her tightly against me, focusing on the feel of her in my arms, trying to stay in *this* moment, with *this* woman. But my memory has taken hold and I feel Maggie's soft exhale against my lips, Maggie rolling under me in the dewy grass, Maggie's mouth connecting with mine.

"I love you too," Krystal says, and I can only faintly make out the words over the sound of the river rushing in my ears.

I am an addict and Maggie Thompson is my drug.

Maggie

Technically, I am trespassing. *Technically,* trespassing is not part of the New Me plan. But it hardly feels like trespassing to use the neighbor's gorgeous, well-maintained pool when a) I've been doing it since I was sixteen, and b) the rich dude who owns the place is never around. I like to think I'm doing him a favor. He must spend a crap ton of money to maintain this place, but he doesn't get any use out of it because he's always away at his house in Vail or wherever. It would be wasteful for me *not* to use it just because of some technicality.

I hoist myself over the gate and feel greedy anticipation. Surrounded by lush landscaping and featuring a cascade of water that circulates from hot tub to pool, the space is more water feature than swimming hole. I don't know Rich Dude, but he has excellent taste, and this little oasis is one of my favorite places on Earth.

I could have headed home after the reception, but I knew I wouldn't sleep tonight. I told my mom I wanted to stay over, and I waited until everyone was in bed before grabbing a robe and trekking across a couple acres of lush grass for a moonlight swim.

I'm no stranger to insomnia, but it's been worse since I returned home. In the silence of the night, there's too much room for my thoughts and they expand until they fill every corner of my mind. While I was away, I could be anyone I wanted to be, but in New Hope, everywhere I turn, someone's labeling me. When I was young, I was just *one of the Thompson girls,* but now the labels aren't so innocuous. *Black sheep. College dropout.*

Slut.

I drop the terry cloth robe from my shoulders and dive into the water completely nude. Most pools would be intolerably cold in Indiana before June, but the water circulating from the hot tub keeps the temperature comfortable from spring to fall. Even if it was cold, I'd still be here. Exercise is the only thing that calms my mind. Tonight, I'll swim laps to escape the demons.

Until last year, small-town life was the only life I'd ever known, so I should be used to it, but you can be cut open a hundred times, and the slice of the blade still hurts.

I just never expected Will to be the one holding the knife.

Does he love her? Would he marry my sister out of spite?

Did he tell Krystal the truth about our canceled vows?

I turn and pull my limbs through the water, asking myself the question I've been avoiding for weeks. *Can I live here and watch Will and Krystal build a life together?*

I count out twenty-five laps. The rhythm of my breathing calms me. The water rushing over my skin salves my wounds. Finally, I rest forearms on the edge of the pool and gulp in air, focusing only on my breath and the water dripping from my face.

"Training for the Olympics?"

I snap my head up in surprise. In the soft glow of the moon, I can make out the bad boy from the reception. He stands in swim trunks three yards from me, a towel draped behind his neck. I was right about the tats. He has some sort of starburst on his left pec, another circling his thick biceps.

"Sneak up on many girls?"

"Only the special ones." He drops the towel on a chair and dives into the water.

When he surfaces, my heart kicks up a beat. He's close. I could almost touch him if I reached out.

But even as my eyes tour his broad chest and sculpted shoulders, I back away. "What are you doing here?"

His eyebrow quirks. "I live here."

I snort. "No you don't." Then, when his expression remains stoic, "Shit. Really? You're Rich Dude?"

"Rich who?" He looks puzzled. And annoyed.

Giggles bubble up and slip past my lips. I've always pictured the owner of this property to be some white-haired old man with a cane and a monocle. Asher is so far off the mark, I can't help my laughter. "Shit. I'm sorry. I just…" I laugh more, and it feels damn good. My muscles are spent from my swim, my mind is calm, and laughing feels like a long-denied decadent treat.

"You haven't come to swim in a long time," he says softly.

That cuts my laughter short. "You watch me?" I want to feel violated by the idea. But the thought of *this* man watching me swim nude in his pool zips potent arousal through my veins.

Asher shakes his head, studying me. "My groundskeeper told me a young girl used to sneak in about once a week. I assume that was you?"

"Yeah," I say softly.

"Why'd you stop?"

"I left town for a while."

"Looking for something?"

I shake my head. "Running away."

He nods, as if my answer is perfectly reasonable, and I get the sense that he doesn't just accept it, he *understands* it. His gaze settles on my mouth. When his eyes drop to the water and my bare breasts, his breath catches, and I feel that rush that comes from being desired, that false sense of worth I'm willing to be fooled by tonight. Suddenly, I want him to kiss me. Touch me. More.

I want to bury my loneliness under the weight of a man's body on mine, to erase unwelcome memories with his mouth.

This man's body. This man's mouth.

"Sorry I had to disappear earlier." His voice is low, husky as he watches me.

"I'd let you make it up to me," I murmur, closing the distance between us. I hesitate, but his gaze—hot, hungry, all over me—is all the invitation I need.

"You've had a long day," he says. "You want to talk?"

I drape my arms behind his neck. "Why would you think I want to talk to you at all?"

He grunts. "Because you're looking at me like a starved woman at a prime rib buffet."

"Yes," I murmur. "What does that have to do with talking?"

His eyes are so damn sexy. The kind of eyes you see in magazines, where the man staring at you from the pages seems to invite you to strip bare while promising you'd enjoy it.

"Don't you want us to get to know each other before you indulge?"

I pretend to consider it. "I'm more about the meal than the conversation."

"You're a kid." If it's supposed to be an objection it rings weak against the pressure of his hand on my hip.

I trace a rivulet of water down his neck. "I'm twenty-one." I bring up my knees and wrap my legs around his waist, satisfied when he draws in his breath with a sharp hiss.

"Is this about him?" he asks.

I frown. "Who?"

"The groom at your sister's wedding? He has some kind of hold on you. I saw it in your eyes. In his."

"This has nothing to do with William Bailey."

He looks unconvinced but doesn't call my bluff. Instead, he brushes his lips over mine. Gentle. Careful. Sweet.

The only thing that can break me tonight is sweet, and I won't be broken. I bite his full bottom lip and dig my nails into his shoulder blades.

A quick study, he gets my message. His hand tangles into my hair while the other digs into my ass and pulls me against him. The hard length of his cock rests between my legs and lights a hot coil of pulsing energy.

He rubs his tongue against mine and moans. Or maybe that's me, because I'm pulling him closer. I wrap my arm tighter behind his neck, and I'm practically crawling up him in my efforts to get closer and *closer* still.

I break the kiss and make myself back off. I'm not the kind of girl who loses control. I don't lose my mind over men and expect to be saved. I don't want Asher to save me.

His fingertips are at my hip, tracing an invisible path down and under, moving ever closer to that coiled ache between my thighs. His lips part and our breath mingles as I savor the heat of his body against mine, the sweet anticipation of his fingers inching closer to where I want them.

I slide a hand down his bare chest and between our bodies and cup him through his swim trunks. I'm rewarded with another hiss and then his lips, his tongue, his teeth, hot and desperate against my neck, nipping, toying, playing. Electrifying the sensitive skin.

He cups my breast, and this time I know the moan I hear is my own.

"So goddamn sexy." His thumb flicks across my nipple, a strangled sound escaping his throat.

I graze my fingertips under the waistband of his swim trunks. I want to feel him in my palm. I want that power to whip through me as I wrap my hands around his hot flesh and it pulses thicker, harder.

For a moment, that's where this is headed. His hands are greedy, all over me, his mouth doing delicious things to my neck.

"You have protection, right?" I ask.

He laughs and stops toying with me, his head leaning against my shoulder. Slowly, he slides his hands to my back. "That's not exactly something I keep tucked in my swim trunks."

I'm so aroused it hurts. Asher is stunning. Solid. Delicious. I want to bite into that corded muscle of his neck. Want to explore that smattering of chest hair with my fingers while I drag my mouth down his flat stomach.

But he doesn't have protection, and that's a deal breaker.

"In your house?" My breathing's unsteady, my heart pounding.

He cups my face in one big hand. "Why don't you run home and get dressed? I'll take you to breakfast."

My jaw goes slack. Who the hell is this guy? Who has brakes that good? "Are you serious? I mean, you don't want to…" Rarely am I at a loss for words.

"Sure, I want to do a lot of things. But sweetheart, you don't know a damn thing about me."

"You're really hung up on that." I unwrap my legs from around him and run a hand over my eyes.

Just my luck that I'd pick a bad boy who's all Mr. Sensitivity and wants to *get to know me.*

So be it. That's a better fit for the New Me plan anyway, right?

"Good. Because, you know, I'm not that kind of girl anyway." I wait a beat, but God doesn't strike me dead. "I'll be back in fifteen minutes?"

His lip twitches.

"What?"

"I've just never met a woman who can really get ready in fifteen minutes."

I hoist myself out of the water. "I'll bet breakfast on it. If I take longer than fifteen minutes, I'll cook for you."

Asher runs his eyes over my body, lingering at all my best parts. "Deal."

I grab my towel, making no effort to minimize the swish of my hips as I exit through his gate for the first time.

I pad through the dewy grass back to my mother's house and slip in the back door. I take a quick shower to wash off the chlorine. After a towel-down and some lotion, I slip into jeans and a tank, and pull my wet hair into a ponytail.

When I head toward the door again, my mom is blocking it. Her arms are crossed and worry creases her features. "Is there something you want to tell me?"

That old shame slithers up my spine and I immediately imagine she knows what I've been up to tonight. The trespassing. The strange man. The lust.

So many deadly sins, so little time.

"I don't live here anymore. I don't need your permission to go to breakfast with a friend."

She looks at her watch skeptically. "It's 3 a.m."

"I'm hungry."

She shakes her head. "I want you to think about how important that wedding was to your sister. And then I want you to think about how you can make it right."

My jaw drops. "What?"

She tucks a piece of chestnut hair behind her ear and cocks her head. "We're a family, Maggie, and we'll forgive you for your mistakes. But we can't do that until you own up to them."

My fists clench until I feel the bite of my nails against my palm. It's a lecture I've heard so many times I could recite it in my sleep. It's a lecture I deserved more times than I can count. "I didn't have anything to do with the stink bomb." The words are hard and gritty, pushed through clenched teeth.

"Maggie—"

I push past her, through the door and into the moonlight, anger and hurt a burning fist in my chest.

When I finally steady myself and make it to Asher's, he's waiting for me on his patio, sipping out of a steaming mug.

"You *lose*."

I tense, still wound up from my confrontation with my mom. "What?"

He smiles and points to his watch. "Twenty-five minutes. You lost the bet." His smile fades. "Are you okay?"

"Oh, right. Yeah." I wave a hand. "I'm fine." I let out a long, slow breath and settle into a chair. The moon shines bright and stars sprinkle across that infinite span of darkness. "I've missed this."

"What? Breakfast? First dates?"

"The stars. The light is constant in the city. Inescapable. I missed seeing the stars," I say, more to myself than him.

Suddenly his words register and I shift my eyes to him. "And this isn't a date."

Asher raises an eyebrow but doesn't question me. "So you left for a while but now you're back…for good?"

I wrinkle my nose. "You still insist on playing the get-to-know-you game?"

"Absolutely." He grins at me and leans forward. "I like hiking, seafood, and long walks on the beach at sunset."

I can't help but smile. "You'd think we had a country full of avid hikers," I say. "Every trail at every national park would be packed if everyone who says they like to hike actually did it."

"Your turn," he says. "Tell me something about yourself."

Is this guy for real?

I steal his mug from his hands and take a long sip of hot, rich coffee. "I'm waiting."

I let the heat sink to my belly and relax my shoulders. "Well, I *should* tell you one thing."

"What's that?"

"I am *that kind of girl*."

His laugh is rich and deep and sexy. "Sure you are."

"You don't believe me? Ask…oh, anyone in this town."

Something changes in his eyes. If sadness had a color I'd say I could see it circling his pupils. "I don't put much stock in the things people say. Anyway, I'd rather hear about you from your lips."

He can't possibly know what that single statement means to me. The silence stretches between us as I consider how to abbreviate my life into a series of simple sentences. He doesn't rush me. Doesn't seem intimidated by silence like so many people are. That alone makes me want to share myself with him.

"I'm just Maggie." I fight the urge to say too much. Months trapped in a self-constructed prison of silence have left me hungry for a confidant, but sexy Asher isn't it. "Black sheep. College dropout. Famished. Painfully turned on."

He groans, a low, guttural sound that speaks to his own arousal. "Well, I can fix the famished part, but the last will have to wait."

But I don't want to wait. I need to…escape. Forget. "I pay my bets." I wrap my fingers around his biceps. "Let me cook for you."

"You really cook?"

My eyes flick to the large French doors at the back of his house, but I dismiss the idea, ready to be on my own turf. "Follow me to my place and I'll show you."

I think we both know I'm not the slightest bit interested in food.

Asher

Maggie takes her coffee black. Straight from the pot, no sweetener, no fancy cream. Just coffee. She puts herself out there in the same way— no frills, no pretense, no bullshit. Just Maggie.

I like that. I like it more than I want to. I like *her* more than I want to. More than I've liked any woman since Juliana fucked me over.

We're at her shitty little rental house in New Hope, and our breakfast dishes litter the kitchen table.

"I've decided I'm not going to sleep with you," she informs me between bites of feta omelet.

"Really?"

"Yeah, my food is so damn good, I don't need you to get off." She takes a sip of coffee. Her tongue darts out to taste her bottom lip after every sip, an innocent gesture that makes me think of mouth and tongue and tasting in a very different context.

"Hmm," I say, as if considering. "You make a damn good omelet, but I promise you I'm better."

"Are you sure?" She slips another bite in her mouth. "Because I'm bordering on foodgasmic about now." Her eyes float closed, and she makes a little sound at the back of her throat, tilting her head back a fraction of an inch.

I put down my fork. In the battle between my throbbing dick and empty stomach, my dick has won. It's not just that she's gorgeous. There are plenty of gorgeous women in this world. Maggie is more than that. She's a study in contradictions and I am an eager student.

My time in New Hope is coming to an end, and I don't know what I was thinking when I joined her in the pool tonight.

That's a lie. I know exactly what I was thinking. I was thinking of big smiles and bright green eyes that are so damn familiar I'm sure I've seen them before. I was thinking of soft skin and bare, sun-kissed shoulders.

I was thinking of the way her face looked by the river when the asshole in the tux told her he was marrying someone else. I didn't understand the conversation. Didn't need to understand it to know she needed me. To feel it.

"Do you make a habit of cooking breakfast for strange men?"

She runs her eyes over me, lingering on my chest and the tat snaking around my biceps. "Only the good-looking ones."

Or only when she's trying to get another man out of her mind. "Are you in school?"

"Not at the moment." She pushes her plate across the table. "Do you want any more? I can make you another."

I'm used to women trying to tell me their life story, trying to play on my sympathies. I'm used to women who want me to rescue them, but not this one. "Is there a reason that you change the subject every time I ask you a personal question?"

She leans back in her chair. "I'm a private person."

My mind is flooded with images—her hair slicked back from her face, her breasts rounded under the surface of the water. When her tongue darted out to taste my lips and she wrapped those long legs behind my back, I lost sight of all sense.

Maggie chews on the corner of her lip and my brain paints a picture of those lips working their way down my stomach, opening over my cock.

"Don't you want to..." she'd asked.

"You didn't seem so private in the pool."

"That was just about sex, Asher."

Another contradiction. That openness. That in-your-face sexuality matched with complete avoidance of any kind of intimacy.

And hell, I could use some just-about-sex right now. It's been too long since I've tasted a woman, since I've felt a woman's mouth on my dick and buried myself inside her.

But I'm not about to end my celibate streak with someone as vulnerable as Maggie. Because no matter what she says, what happened in the pool wasn't just about sex. It was about *him*. The groom. The man her eyes kept returning to as we danced.

"You want to meet my little girl?" Her words rip me from my reverie.

"You have a kid?" Where are all the toys? There are dog toys all over the place, but no signs of a baby doll or Barbie.

Maggie would probably hang by that thick red hair before she'd let a child of hers play with Barbie dolls. But what about Little People or picture books? I hope she's not one of those moms who always pawns her kid off on the sitter. That makes me uncomfortable as hell.

Then, like a fucking genius, I put it all together. "Your little girl is a dog, isn't she?"

Maggie hops up from her chair and tugs the back door open. "Come on, baby girl. It's okay. Lucy! Come say hi to Mama!"

I love the idea of this rough woman owning a spoiled little dog.

The image in my mind is turned on its head when one hundred and fifty pounds of Rottweiler runs toward Maggie with the frenzied glee of a ten-pound pup.

When Lucy reaches Maggie's feet, she immediately drops to the ground and rolls onto her back.

"I should have known," I mutter.

"What?"

"I should have known you'd have a big-ass guard dog to match your big-ass guard dog personality."

Maggie scoffs. "Lotta good she does me. Lucy's the biggest coward I've ever met. Aren't you, sweetie?" she coos to the dog, rubbing on her belly. Lucy writhes in pleasure.

"So you *don't* have any kids?"

Maggie stands and the dog cowers behind her legs. "It's just me and Lucy here."

I drop to my knees and extend a hand. "Come here, sweetie."

Lucy howls in half excited whine, half terrified cry.

"We're still getting used to each other," Maggie explains. "I adopted her from the shelter when I moved back to town last month."

I'm still waiting with my hand out, but I flick my eyes up to Maggie. "Most people would have gotten a puppy."

"That's why Lucy needed me." Her eyes go soft as she studies her dog and she adds, quietly, "I needed her too."

Finally, Lucy edges toward me.

Maggie gapes. "You've got to be freaking kidding me!"

I shrug. Lucy drops to the floor at my feet, rolling to her back so I can rub her belly. "Dogs like me."

"Lucy's afraid of everyone. Even my *mom*."

"Maybe your mom's scary."

She snorts. "You have no idea." Then she grabs my hand and pulls me up. "I can't have her liking you more than me."

Her face is inches from mine and something's nagging at the back of my mind again. Do I know this woman? Maybe I saw her around town during my rare visits to my river house before this year, but the recognition, the *déjà vu* I feel when I look at her is something more.

Her skin is fresh and clear. Freckles scatter across the bridge of her nose. And I swear she smells like clean laundry hanging to dry in the summer sun.

Fuck. I'm in trouble.

"Let me take you out sometime, Maggie."

"I don't play games." She says it in a husky whisper that makes me think of lazy Sunday mornings in a warm bed, the sun slanting in on us as we explore each other's bodies.

"Who said I'm playing a game?"

"Isn't that what dating is?" Her eyes drop to my lips. "If I want something, I take it."

"And you think you want me?"

A smile spreads across her face. "Why don't you come find out?" She cocks her head and walks toward the hallway.

I follow like a smitten fool.

She leans against a doorframe and pulls her tank over her head, revealing creamy skin, heavy breasts in a simple black bra. No lace. No frills. And so damn sexy. I can still feel the weight of them, slick with pool water, her pebbled nipple against my palm, her breath quickening against my neck.

"Maggie, what are you doing?"

"I haven't figured out all the details yet, but I figure we can play it by ear. We have"—she glances over her shoulder to the clock—"approximately five hours before I need to play the good daughter for a family brunch at my mom's house."

The shirt drops from her fingers to the floor, and I groan involuntarily as she moves to the button on her jeans. I stop her hands with one of mine.

"Oh, sorry." She looks up, laughter in her eyes. "Did you want to do it?"

She has no idea. I could do it. I could fuck her today and forget her tomorrow. No one would be surprised. Half the world thinks I'm a selfish asshole, so why not prove them right?

"I'm not going to sleep with you, Maggie. Not yet."

Her eyes narrow. "I told you I don't play games. I'm not about that."

"And I don't make a habit of screwing women who are hung up on other men."

"I don't see any other men here, do you?" Her lips curve in amusement.

She shimmies out of her jeans, watching me as she steps out of them. She's in nothing but her bra and a black scrap of thong. I fist my hands against the temptation to trace the curve of her hip, tighten my jaw against the need to press my open mouth against the flat of her belly.

Grabbing the doorframe, I take a deep breath.

"I'm going to jump in the shower." Maggie pulls the tie from her hair and a thick curtain of red falls around her shoulders. "I'd love some company, but you do what you must."

She disappears around the corner and I count backwards from ten.

Ten. Nine...

Ancient plumbing squeals and the shower kicks on. I imagine her under the spray, all that soft, pale skin slick with water.

Eight. Seven. Six...

It would be so easy to follow her, so easy to pretend I didn't see that pain in her eyes.

Five. Four...

But I'm so damn drawn to her already. She has this magnetic pull on me.

Three. Two...

This lust is so powerful it nearly has me snarling with need.

One. I won't slide inside of her while her mind is full of another man. Been there. Done that.

Turning around and walking out the door is on my top ten list of hardest things I've ever had to do.

chapter three

Maggie

MY EYES are heavy. Even amidst the constant chitchat of the Thompson family luncheon, I can't stop yawning.

Before I left my house for brunch, I found Asher's number on my kitchen table, a note scribbled under it.

Call me when you're ready for that date.

"Isn't this fun?" my mom asks me now. People are milling around with low-calorie mimosas and chattering about Krystal's wedding, but the guest of honor is fashionably late, as always.

Fun? It is the final day of a torturous three days. Rehearsal dinner Friday, Krystal's wedding yesterday, and today a lunch at the Thompson house with people so distantly related it would be legal for us to marry in most states. Fun would have been Asher joining me in the shower. I stayed under the spray of the water for a solid twenty minutes before accepting that he wasn't going to join me. *Sadist.*

Mom folds her arms. "I wanted to talk to you about your date last night. Some scruffy bum with piercings is the most respectable man you could find for your sister's wedding?" She shakes her head. "Where'd you even find him?"

I shrug. "Just wandering down by the river."

"You're not funny," she hisses.

I bite my tongue. I came home to begin Operation New Me, which includes a better relationship with my mother. She doesn't appreciate my "sass," as she calls it.

Gran waddles toward me. The scent of her makes me smile. Lavender soap and whiskey. "I had a vision during my meditation yesterday."

Mom nudges Gran. "Your devil games aren't welcome here." She produces a tube of lipstick from her pocket. "Just one coat, Margaret. People will think you have no self-respect."

Granny slaps at her hand. "Leave the girl alone!"

I roll my eyes.

"Maggie," Granny continues, "your past is going to visit you and bring your future as a gift."

I try to look interested. I love Gran, even if I think her brand of spirituality is a little kooky. "That's…profound."

"Are you seeing anyone, Maggie?" My mother's voice is low, the whisper reserved for talk of scandal—like premarital cohabitation and non-procreative sex. "Are you even *trying* to find love? Or do you intend to continue fornicating with random men outside the sanctity of marriage?"

"So if I were married I'd have your blessing to *fornicate* with random men? Maybe I should reconsider my stance on marriage." The words are out of my mouth before I can stop them. I'm batting zero on the New Me plan.

"Margaret Marie!" Mom's scowl is so fierce, it threatens to bust through the Botox. "Watch your mouth this instant! I do hope you still go to confession."

"Maggie's on a spiritual journey, Gretchen," Granny defends.

I frown. That's what Gran says about her crazy clients, and I don't want to be categorized with them.

"You need to let her find her own way," Granny continues. "But Maggie, your aura does seem terribly dark. You should come to my office sometime this week and we can do a cleansing."

"My aura can't help it, Gran. It feels fat in anything but black."

Granny grins. "Clever girl."

I'm quickly reaching my fill of family togetherness.

"So, Maggie," Aunt—Sally? Sophie?—asks, "you're getting married, right? When is your wedding, again?"

The other aunt shoots the first a hard glare. "Don't you remember?" Then to me, "Did it bother you to see him marry someone else, dear?"

I grit my teeth.

"It must be hard to see someone you once planned to marry fall in love with your sister."

As if mentioning her summoned the devil, Krystal bursts into the room, bringing the hot breath of Indiana summer with her.

"I'm so sorry I'm late!" she says, waving a hand in front of her red-tinged cheeks.

A bright-eyed blonde claps her hands. "Of course you're late after your *wedding night.*"

Krystal smiles at her friend and shakes her head. "Will and I never made it official yesterday. It just didn't feel right to let someone else control our day. We appreciate everything you all did this weekend, and we hope you'll join us when we try again later in the summer."

The chatter screeches to a halt. Damn it. Now they're all staring at me.

My sister Lizzy comes over to stand by my side.

"I'm so happy for you both," I manage, but I can't bring myself to exhale until they stop looking at me.

When everyone finally returns to their conversations, Granny leans over the table. "Are you okay?"

"I'm fine, Gran. It really doesn't bother me. My relationship with Will is over, and I'm okay with that."

Granny nods, but it's clear by her expression that she's unconvinced.

"You're really okay?" Lizzy whispers this time.

Across the room, Hanna gives me a pitying half-smile.

"Okay, no," I admit. "I'm not fine. But only because I don't want people looking at me like Hanna is right now."

One of Krystal's friends is asking about her wedding night in a stage whisper as clear as her wriggling eyebrows. "We're going to wait until it's official," Krystal says with a hand pressed to her chest.

"That's my girl," my mom says with an approving nod.

I stifle the urge to snort. Maybe Krystal hasn't had sex with Will, but she's no virgin.

"You need to settle a bet for us," Lizzy tells me as our server settles three chocolate martinis on our table. "Was that *Asher Logan* you were dancing with at the wedding last night?"

"It wasn't," Hanna says. "Though he's a dead ringer for him." She hums and—

"Did you just lick your lips?" I narrow my eyes at my sisters. I can't remember if he ever told me his last name. "How do you know Asher?"

Hanna's jaw drops. "No way!"

Lizzy hides her smile behind her martini. "Apparently they're on a first-name basis."

With a French-tipped nail, Lizzy tucks a long lock of blond hair behind her ear. Tonight, she's dressed to kill in a pale pink strapless, show-off-the-legs-that-go-for-miles dress. Next to her, Hanna is dressed a bit more modestly in a black capris and a lavender sweater set. She's as drop-dead gorgeous as her twin, if in a different way. Since good daughters spend time with their family, martini night with the twins is part of Operation New Me. So far it's been my favorite part of my ill-conceived plan.

"I just met him last night," I explain. "How do *you* know him?"

The girls giggle.

"How do we *know* Asher Logan?" Lizzy asks.

"Asher 'Sexy Beast' Logan?" Hanna adds.

I fold my arms. "That's what I asked."

The girls exchange a look.

"She's clueless," Lizzy mutters.

"He was only the hottest lead singer in the history of rock bands," Hanna says.

"But Maggie was always more into that angry chick music."

I wave a hand in front of them. "Hello. Quit talking about me like I'm not here."

Lizzy narrows her eyes. "You really didn't know?"

"All I know is that he is the Rich Dude who owns the house next door to Mom."

"Shut up!" Hanna's eyes go wide. "Asher Logan lives next door to Mom?"

Lizzy's eyes light up. "I take back every bad thing I ever said about New Hope."

"If the Asher I was dancing with last night is the Asher you're talking about, then yes, he owns the house next to mom's. But I don't think he *lives* there, or if he does I don't think he has for long."

Lizzy downs her martini. "This is so huge." She waves to the waitress. "I'm gonna need another."

"We need details," Hanna says, leaning forward.

"I met him at Krystal's wedding. He was down by the river and I thought he was a lost wedding guest." I snort, realizing for the first time why he was really there. "But I guess he was just in his own backyard."

Hanna grins. "Yeah, because Mom's backyard is right next to *Asher Logan's* backyard. God, this is epic."

Lizzy waves her hands excitedly, urging me to share more. "So you met at the wedding. And then?"

"We talked, danced. We ran into each other after the reception was over."

"Where? Did Maggie go out carousing?" Lizzy presses her palms into the table. "It's finally happened. Hell froze over."

I roll my eyes. "I hardly went out carousing. He caught me swimming in his pool and…things happened."

Hanna wilts. "If you tell me you got to have hot pool sex with Asher 'Sexier Than God' Logan, I may never forgive you."

"Right, but that's just it. We didn't have sex. We messed around, and then I took him back to my place for breakfast and took off my clothes."

"And this is a problem because…?" Lizzy quirks a brow. "You're not thinking of changing your naughty girl ways on us are you? Has Mom's constant harassment finally broken you? Because, seriously, Maggie—if Asher Logan is in the picture, now is *not* the time."

"No. He rejected me. Told me he wanted to *get to know me.*"

"*Oh,*" the girls chorus. Judging by the disappointment on their faces, you'd think they were the ones left high and dry.

"Yeah. What the hell?"

Lizzy throws back her head and laughs, a full-stomach laugh that has everyone in the bar looking at us.

I scowl. "It's not funny."

She's doesn't even attempt to stifle her damn giggles of delight. "Yes, yes it is."

Hanna nods. "It kind of is, Mags."

"It's not like I go after one-night stands often, but the few times I have I've never been *denied*. Now I know how guys must feel."

"Maybe he's gay," Lizzy says.

"That would be a tragedy," Hanna whimpers.

Lizzy nudges her. "Don't be so narrow-minded. Gay boys deserve hot men too."

I roll my eyes. "He's not gay. Trust me. His attraction was physically evident."

"Oh, yeah?" Lizzy props her chin on her hands. "How's he measure up?"

I groan. "Why the hell do you think I took him back to my place and stripped down to my skivvies while he was trying to get out the door?" If I wanted Asher to distract me, I was successful because I can't stop thinking about him.

I smile into my chocolate martini, wondering if the girls would be offended if I tainted "Martini Night" with a beer.

I am nothing like my sisters. They do things like have makeover parties and martini nights. They ooze femininity from every pore, from their hair to their designer jeans and Gucci heels. Me? I'm all about comfort and practicality. My favorite outfit consists of worn Levi's and a ribbed tank top, and I'm convinced that heels are medieval torture devices. The girls primp and fuss, and make semi-annual shopping trips to the Big Apple, whereas I have discovered I can make a twenty-dollar dress from Target look damn good.

"You still got more action than I did," Lizzy says. "I was trying to hook up with that groomsman. You know, Will's friend from college?"

Hanna snorts. "He's not into girls."

Lizzy frowns. "A tragedy."

"Gay boys deserve hot men too," Hanna says, parroting Lizzy's words right back at her.

"I guess," Lizzy pouts. "Did you see Krystal's eyes today? I think she cried a lot last night."

"Poor thing," Hanna says. "Who do you think did it?"

Probably by some bored kid with nothing better to do with his Saturday. "I don't know. I figure it'll remain a mystery."

"Hmm," Lizzy says, "like the mystery of who stole those fraternity boys' clothes the night they went skinny dipping in Lake Lemon?"

I can't help but smile at the memory from my first semester at Sinclair. All those beautiful men searching for their clothes in the moonlight.

"Or the mystery of how the Sigmas all came down with stomach cramps after outing your friend Ed?"

Her implication clicks into place in my mind and I lift my hands, palms up. "You think *I* did this?"

The girls shake their heads, saying "Oh, no! Not us" in unison.

"Why would I want to ruin Krystal's wedding with a stink bomb?"

"*We* don't think you would," Lizzy says. "It's just..."

"There's been some talk," Hanna finishes.

"And your name's been mentioned," Lizzy says.

Hanna pats my arm. "It's no mystery how much you hate weddings."

Translation: Everyone knows how much I must hate seeing Will marry Krystal.

"We'd hate weddings too if—" Lizzy cuts herself off.

Hanna finishes for her. "You know."

"I do"—I soften the truth—"*dislike* weddings, but not because—"

"Of course not," the girls chorus.

"I would never—"

Lizzy holds up her hand. "You don't have to say anything else. I guess it just occurred to Hanna and me..."

Hanna nods. "...With the talk and all..."

"...How insensitive it was for Krystal to ask you to be in her wedding after..."

"You know," they say together.

"It's fine. I'm the one who canceled the wedding. I don't have any hold on Will."

"Was it weird?" Lizzy asks in a whisper. "Being a bridesmaid in Will's wedding?"

Hanna bites her lip and watches me.

"So, Asher's some sort of rock star?" I ask to change the subject.

Lizzy huffs, unimpressed by my non-sequitur, but Hanna's drawn in by more talk of the sexy rocker and gapes at me in dismay. "The *lead singer* of Infinite Gray?"

"Infinite Gray?" I frown. "Isn't that the band that put out the song 'Unbroken?'" I listened to that song on repeat during my sophomore year of high school, but then...I don't remember anything else. One-hit wonders? "A rock star," I mutter, trying to fit it all into place. There was something familiar about Asher—those *eyes*. This must be why.

"Former rock star," Lizzy corrects. "The band dissolved after their first tour. Same old story—hit the big time too young and got caught up in booze and drugs."

"I heard," Hanna says, "that he beat the shit out of some dude in a bar last year and got tried for aggravated battery."

My jaw goes slack. Now I really do want that beer. *Aggravated battery.* "Really?"

Hanna bites her lip. "No one but Asher knows what really happened that night. I'm sure he's a nice guy."

Right. Because nice guys get charged with aggravated battery all the time.

"Doesn't matter anyway, right?" I shake my head and force a smile. "He's had that house for, what, five years? And this is the first time we've seen him around? It's not like I think I'm going to see him again."

chapter four

William

THE BEST part of living in a small town is that everyone knows everyone. This is also the shittiest part of living in a small town, a fact I'm reminded of every time I take my grandmother to her bi-weekly salon visits.

"I'm so glad you're okay," Cecilia says as Grandma gets situated in her chair. "It's just terrible what they did to your wedding, Willy."

I cringe but don't bother to correct her on my name. Cecilia has been calling me Willy since I was a toddler. If my red-cheeked embarrassment didn't stop her when I was a teenager, a polite objection isn't going to stop her now.

"I think it was that Maggie," Grandma says with a knowing nod. "She didn't want to see you marrying her sister."

"Grandma." My voice is hard, making Grandma's shoulders drop, her face go sad. "Maggie wouldn't do that," I say, softer now, because as much as I hate the way she talks about Maggie, I know it's all out of love for me.

Grandma shakes her head. "That's what you said when I told you about the rumors back in high school. Then the truth came out. It always does. Poor Ann Quimby's whole life was torn apart by the girl."

"Mom, she's the county *prosecutor* now and has a new husband and children. I think she survived."

Gran turns to Cecilia and whispers, "Boy's got no sense when it comes to that little girl."

Cecilia shakes her head and combs her fingers through Grandma's hair.

I let out a slow breath. "Grandma, I have my cell. Just give me a call when you're done." I head to the door before they have a chance to say anything else about the wedding or Maggie or gossip that should have died years ago.

When I hit the sidewalk, I'm swarmed by the greetings of the bookstore patrons next door. They're sitting out on the patio, sipping coffee and sharing "local news," more easily recognizable as gossip.

"So sorry to hear about your wedding, Willy," Mrs. White calls.

I close my eyes. God *damn* do I hate when people call me that. "It's okay," I assure her, forcing a smile. "What matters is that we have each other. No stink bomb can change that."

"Of course it can't, and Krystal's mother tells us you're opening an art gallery in the old Beatlemeyer building."

"He is?" the woman across from her croons. "Well, that's what we need around here. More young people investing in this town. Putting roots down. Good for you, young man. Not like all those snotty college kids running away as soon as they get their degree."

"Thank you," I say. "We're lucky to be in a position to do it."

I excuse myself, but I don't turn to my car. The Curl Up and Dye sits just three blocks off campus and I need the walk to clear my head.

New Hope is simultaneously a young and aging community. The largest population is our community of seniors who lived and worked in this little town their whole life. Our second largest population comes from Sinclair, a small liberal arts college that families all over the country spend a small fortune to send their spoiled, privileged children to. In between, there are a few of us staying for jobs at the college or family ties or, in my case, both.

I can't leave Grandma. The woman raised me and she doesn't have anyone else. So I'm here with Krystal, and we are going to make the most of it.

My steps slow as I approach the county library and my breath catches in my throat.

At a seat by the window, Maggie sits with her laptop open, headphones on, and a soft smile on her lips. My feet stall under me as she leans toward her screen and her smile grows.

Suddenly, she turns to the window, and our gazes lock through the glass. Her smile falls away.

My chest is heavy with regret and longing and...fuck, I'm *angry*. She's the one who left. She's the one who called it off.

So why does she look at me like I've broken her heart?

Maggie

I might as well be sixteen again, I'm so obsessed with Infinite Gray.

I made a little trip to my local library to use their internet access—because Operation New Me means I can't steal it from my neighbors anymore—and now my hard drive is loaded with the band's album and a couple dozen half-nude pictures of Asher. The more I listened to the album, the more the memories came back—my ceiling fan spinning above my bed, my heart frozen in my chest, that low, mellow voice crooning from my MP3 player as I did my damndest to sink into my numbness and disintegrate into nothing.

"Come back and break me, don't let this go unspoken. I'm numb when I'm whole and you left me unbroken."

And the pictures? Dear God. If I had been the kind of teenager who watched music videos instead of the kind who broke her father's heart, I never would have forgotten that face or body. Turns out half-naked pictures of a rock star dubbed "Sexy Beast" are plentiful. Thank you, Internets. But there still weren't enough. Not when you consider how when I close my eyes I can feel his muscles flexing under my fingers, still taste his salty skin on my tongue.

I pack up my laptop and head to the parking lot with a sigh. I just wasted half a day obsessing over a rock star who will never sleep with me. Maybe I am sixteen again.

Stepping out of the library, I squint into the setting sun and see Asher "Sexy Beast" Logan leaning against my car.

My steps stutter and his lips curl into a grin as he looks me over.
Play it cool.

"Your wife kick you out, Pretty Boy?"

He looks damn fine standing there, his dark shades blocking his eyes from the setting sun, a tiny silver hoop glinting in each ear. He is all hard muscle and tan in his fitted black t-shirt and faded jeans. I always said there's no man as hot as my car. Now I'm not so sure.

My first thought is that we could be naked and in my bed in twenty minutes. My second is of the story Lizzy just told me, a story that makes Asher the worst kind of bad boy—capital B, capital N, Bad News.

I pull my keys from my purse. "What are you doing here?"

His too-goddamn-perfect mouth quirks into that cocky half grin. "I wanted to see you."

"Aw! That's what all my stalkers say."

He chuckles. "You owe me a date."

"How'd you even know to find me here?"

"How'd you get the cash for such a sweet ride?"

I drive a deep blue Mustang GT, a gift from my granny. She's terrible with money and we love her for it.

"Marry an old man for his money?" he asks.

"Sure. But I was screwing his brains out when he died, so he didn't mind much."

His smile never wavers. "I want to take you out."

"We discussed this already," I say, my traitorous gaze dipping back to the bulge of his biceps. *Lord have mercy.* "I don't do dates."

"So we'll call it something else," he says. "Try not to get hung up on semantics."

"And what if I say no?"

Asher's smirk should piss me off. This is a man who gets what he wants, and it's written all over his face.

I sigh. "Fine, but only if you have a signed note from your wife that says it's okay if you play with others."

"It's one night. What? Are you afraid you can't resist me?"

Damn. That's a challenge. "Dinner," I say, punching my key fob to unlock my doors. "But none of this macho, He-Man, I-drive-the-lady crap. I have free will and I like to keep my vehicle at my disposal. You might be hot, and I might be joining you for a meal, but you don't own me."

"Are you done?"

I try to stop the smile that's coming, but I can't resist. I don't meet many men willing to call me on my bullshit. "Yeah."

"Do you like Cajun food, loud atmosphere, a good beer list?"

I look him up and down again—a visual journey that is worth it every time. "Goddamn, Asher. You keep going and I might just think you had my number. Cajun Jack's?"

"I'll see you there." He heads toward his Jeep. When he turns back to slide his eyes over my body, I have to tell myself that the heat rushing through me is only a product of the scorching May afternoon sun.

"You're staring at me," I protest between bites of crawfish etouffee.

Asher lifts a shoulder. "Just watching in case you get foodgasmic again."

I hum as I swallow a particularly decadent bite. "I'm close. You like to watch, huh?"

His pupils dilate and his jaw goes a little slack as his gaze drops to my mouth. Just like that, we're not talking about food anymore. Maybe we never were.

I take a sip of my beer to cool off the heat his eyes send through me. Asher isn't drinking. He didn't explain and I didn't ask, but I'm curious. He doesn't strike me as a straight-edger. Hell, he's a former rocker. Maybe he prefers something with a little more punch than beer.

Jack's is slow tonight, and it will be until classes start up at Sinclair in the fall. New Hope is a tiny little town of contrasts—a bizarre mix of yuppie affluence and rural simplicity. The businesses within a two-block radius of campus cater to the private school students—a gourmet coffee shop, an Aveda hair salon, a sushi bar. Outside of those two blocks, residents are served with gas stations that advertise "Live Bait" on their marquees and greasy spoon restaurants where the closest thing to fresh sushi is the fried catfish—locally caught, cleaned, battered, and fried.

"So did you grow up in New Hope?"

"You want to know why I hate dating?" I counter. He frowns and I hold up a hand before he can protest. "I hate dating because dating protocol requires I keep it positive, that I feed you some bullshit about how my childhood was wholesome and awesome blah-blah-bullshit-blah."

He folds his arms on the table and leans forward. "It's a date, Maggie. Not a job interview." When I just stare in response, he says, "My childhood was shitty. I was poor. My dad was a drunk. He put his hands on my mom, and then, when I was old enough by whatever fucked-up standards he had, he put them on me."

"I…" What do you say? "I'm sorry."

He shrugs. "I'm grown now. I have more money than I know what to do with, Mom's all right, and the son of a bitch is dead. Life's not so bad after all."

I let out a breath. Something about Asher compels me to open up. Something about the way his blue eyes take me in. It's like he sees something good when he looks at me, and I want to throw my ugliness in his face to prove him wrong.

I take a long draw from my beer. "I grew up in New Hope," I say in answer to his question. "And I stayed here for college at Sinclair. I probably should have gone away but there's a good art program here." *And Will,* I thought, remembering how Will's decision to come home for graduate school had solidified mine to do undergrad at Sinclair.

"So you're a brain," he says.

I laugh. "In my family, you don't have a choice. Good grades, good behavior, good fashion sense. It's all expected." I realize I've said more than I want to, so I wave it away. "Not that I was ever any good at any of those. Not anything other than painting, actually."

"When do you graduate?"

"Well, I dropped out last year, so that all depends on whether or not they'll take me back."

He exhales sharply. "Fuck, what a relief."

"What?"

"Well"—he starts ticking off reasons on his fingers—"you're gorgeous and sexy and smart. It's intimidating until you throw in the college dropout stuff. I was ready to find a new date."

"*I'm* intimidating? You're the freaking rock star at the table."

Some of the humor drains from his face, but he keeps his smile in place. "You know about that, huh?"

"My sisters told me. You could have mentioned you're in a band."

"I *was* in a band." He wipes his hands on his napkin and shrugs. "Past tense."

With a dreamy sigh, I prop my chin on my fists. "Who knew that one day I'd be on a date with the lead singer from a famous boy band?"

He scowls. "Infinite Gray was not a *boy band*."

"Were there any girls in the band?"

"No."

"That makes you a boy band."

"It made us an all-male rock group."

I bite back my smile. He's so cute when he's irritated. "Right, like 'N Sync."

He winces. "*Not* like 'N Sync. Jesus, watch where you hurl those things. Words hurt, Maggie."

I giggle.

He glowers. "You need a musical intervention."

I perk up. "Ooh! Are you going to make me a playlist?"

"Maybe."

I laugh again, but this time a little snort pops out, making me laugh harder.

He narrows his eyes. "You're playing me, aren't you?"

"Sorry. I couldn't resist."

"So you don't need that playlist?"

"Says who? No boy has ever made a playlist especially for me before. *Please*?"

"Not even in high school?"

That takes some of the wind out of my sails. "I wasn't that kind of girl."

He studies me for a minute and just when I think he's going to dig, he drops it. "Okay. It's your turn. Ask me anything."

I study him for a moment. The ice-blue eyes that keep dropping to my mouth. The stubble I can still feel against my neck. When I finally speak, it's to ask, "What do you have against a perfectly good shower?"

He releases a burst of laughter. "If I'd let you have your way with me, you wouldn't be sitting here with me tonight."

"Oh, you think I would have moved on to another rock star in my long line of rock stars?"

He shrugs.

"You know how much you can hurt a girl's ego by turning her down when she's stripped in front of you?" I put my hand to my chest. "I'll probably be in counseling for months to repair the damage."

"Somehow I think you can handle it."

"Games," I mutter. "Emotionally speaking, I'm going to be the man in this relationship, aren't I?"

"You certainly aren't like any woman I've ever met before."

"Thank God," I say, but my cheeks warm because I know he means it as a compliment. I try damn hard not to care what people think about me, but with Asher, I care. And that worries me.

He pays the bill and we walk out into the dusky evening. When he takes my hand, I don't pull away.

"How do you feel about weddings?" I hear myself ask.

"Proposing already?" He cuts his eyes to me. "I don't know. Seems like we're moving a little fast."

I bite back my smile. "I need an escort."

"To a wedding?"

"To my sister Krystal's wedding. I mean, if you're still in town or whatever. I'm not asking that you make a special trip."

He quirks a brow. "I thought she already got married."

"She wants a do-over. But don't worry, she promises it's going to be *fah-bu-lous*."

He's silent. Can you blame him? He didn't want to sleep with me, and I think *this* is a more appealing proposition?

"Sure," he finally says. "I'd be happy to accompany you."

"Really? Because there's a pretty good chance the twins might maul you at the reception."

He chuckles and cuts his eyes to me. "I can handle a couple of fan girls. Anyway, I know you wouldn't ask me if you didn't feel like you needed to have a date. I've never said no to a woman in need."

"Humph," I snort. "My experience says otherwise."

A block away, a pickup screeches forward at the traffic light, and a guy in a ball cap sticks his head and chest out the window and points at me. "Looooose!" he calls out into the night, drawing out the word. "Loooos-eeee!"

The word, once a sharp knife, is now the sawing of a dull blade against my calloused heart. The truck screeches down the road, and hatred clogs my throat and blocks any response.

"Lucy?" Asher asks. "Isn't that your dog's name?"

Suddenly, I'm overwhelmed by my own naiveté. I really thought I could come back to this godforsaken hole-in-the-earth town and live a normal life? New Hope will never offer me *normal*. If I live and die in New Hope, I imagine they'll carve my tombstone with the word *loose*.

I swallow down my anger and shake my head. "*Loose*," I explain. "As in *loose woman. Promiscuous. Slut.*"

Asher's breath draws in with a raspy hiss and his nostrils flare. Those blue eyes burn as he looks after the offender. He's long gone now, and I'm glad because the look in Asher's eyes says what he'd like to do to them. It should scare me, given his reputation, but instead it helps the insult roll off my back.

I can handle the nastiness now. But I wish I could send Asher back in time to be indignant on behalf of my fifteen-year-old self. She wasn't so hardened.

"Can you tell me a name?" he asks, his voice low and deadly steady.

"They're just stupid townies from my high school." I press my hand to his arm. "It doesn't matter."

He doesn't call me on my lie, but we both know it *does* matter. What had he said in there? *Words hurt.*

He takes my hand and walks me to my car, toying with my fingers.

"Assholes notwithstanding," I whisper, "I had a good time."

"Me too." He rubs the inside of my palm. Soft. Gentle. This man may look rough with his tattoos and piercings, but there is nothing rough about the way he treats me. And, where the violence that flashed in his eyes didn't scare me, this gentleness does.

"Listen," I say. "About the other morning, I just—"

He cuts me off with his mouth. He touches his lips to mine, and I feel frozen for a moment—I am the statue I once trained myself to be. But his mouth is soft and slow and patient. I melt into him, curl my fingers into his chest, slide my tongue against his.

It's the kind of kiss I dreamed about as a girl and never got.

When he pulls away, he traces his thumb over my bottom lip.

"Come home with me?" I ask, breathless from his kiss, his touch.

"You're so damn sweet."

That gets me right in the solar plexus. Men call me *hot*. Men call me *sexy*. Men don't call me *sweet*.

"For a woman who claims to be an open book, you hide so much." He runs his thumb down the side of my neck, over the hollow in my collarbone. "Next time you strip for me, you're taking off more than your clothes."

I step back. "Goodnight, Asher." I climb in my car and drive away—from him and from this aching inside my chest that feels a whole lot like falling.

chapter five

William

MAGGIE THOMPSON is wandering around my art gallery, lips parted, eyes wide. At first, I think I'm imagining it. After all, this place was her dream too. We were going to get married and open New Hope's first art gallery. We'd sell her paintings and my photography. We'd feature Sinclair faculty and students. We'd sell art that people wanted to put in their homes. We'd get a liquor license and serve wine and champagne for clients to sip as they studied the selections and made their choice. And tucked into a corner of the back office we'd keep a bassinet.

My stomach lurches and my breath leaves me in a rush. My gut aches where the memory sucker punched me.

I must have made a noise because Maggie lifts her head and stares at me, mouth in a perfect, surprised circle. And I want to kiss it. Fucking scum of the earth *addict*, I can hardly think of anything but tasting her.

My fingers curl around the loft railing, and I force them to relax, force myself to walk down the stairs and greet her.

"Hi," I say as I hit the last step.

She looks around again. The gallery doesn't officially open for a couple of weeks, and it hasn't been staged yet. Paintings are propped against the walls; sculptures sit in odd groupings.

When she returns her eyes to mine, awkwardness sits between us like a chaperone with too many elbows. I hate it, and I hate myself for thinking about how it felt to hold her together, how it felt to be the thing she needed most in this world, her rock.

"Maggie," I repeat. My voice is a little hard this time, as if it's her fault I can't just let it go. "What are you doing here?"

She swallows audibly. "Sorry, I…" She shakes her head. "There was a flyer in the art building about a summer internship at a new gallery, and I…" She takes a step back. "I should go."

"No. Don't." I don't even realize I've reached for her until my hand touches her arm. The moment that electric zip of contact zings through me, I recoil. "You don't have to go." But even as I say it, I'm backing up, trying to put distance between us.

The click of heels echoes through the cavernous space.

"Hi, Krystal," Maggie says softly, a sad smile on her face.

I clear my throat. "Maggie's here about the internship I advertised on campus."

Krystal's face brightens and she claps her hands together. "Perfect!" she says at the same time Maggie says, "I didn't realize…What?"

Krystal looks between us. "Maggie's good at this stuff—right, Will? And between moving into the new house and planning the second wedding, you need someone you don't have to babysit."

"Krystal," Maggie says, "I don't think…"

Krystal raises a brow, waiting for Maggie to finish. When she doesn't, Krystal turns to me. "I don't see any problem with it, do you?"

"Maggie would do a good job," I acknowledge.

"It's settled, then." She smiles, but I can see the strain around her once soft eyes.

"I'll think about it," Maggie says, edging toward the exit. "I'll let you know. Thank you."

When the door closes behind her, Krystal's smile falters.

"Is this supposed to be some sort of test?" I ask.

She wraps her arms around herself. "Why would you say that?"

I stare at her. The tension between us isn't something we're used to, and neither of us knows how to deal with it, how to fit it into the previously comfortable territory of our relationship.

"Anyway, I'm not worried about her. That guy she was with at the wedding is some sort of rock star. Rumor has it he's cozying up to Lucy."

I set my jaw. "Don't. Call. Her. That."

She takes a step toward me and runs her eyes over my body. "My sister isn't a fifteen-year-old who needs the big, bad college boy anymore, Will. This isn't high school, and you two aren't going to live happily ever after, so stop trying to relive the past."

"Who are you?" The Krystal I fell in love with was never this cold, never this hard, not even when it came to Maggie—*especially* when it came to Maggie.

She's unbuttoning my pants with one hand and cupping me in the other.

I step back, evading her touch and escaping her ugliness. Only then do I see the tears glistening in her eyes.

"If you can't handle her taking some stupid part-time summer internship in this gallery," she says softly, hands hanging limply at her sides, "if that's too much of a fucking temptation for you, then we shouldn't be getting married."

She walks away and I'm left with the uncomfortable truth of her words.

"My sister isn't a fifteen-year-old who needs the big, bad college boy anymore."

I never realized how much I needed Maggie to need me. Until she didn't.

Maggie

I'm torn from a fitful sleep and bolt upright at the sounds of a baby's cries.

I stumble out of bed, fighting free of my tangled sheets, tripping over my own feet. I'm halfway down the hallway before I realize my mistake, but the cries from my dream seem so real they echo in my ears.

Silent, tearless sobs rattle my chest and bring me to my knees.

I crawl toward my bedside table, to the anxiety medication I keep in my purse. Better to stay ahead of it, better to take the meds at the first signs of panic than to let the anxiety grab ahold of me with its sticky, suffocating hands.

I snatch the purse and dump the contents. A white slip of paper flutters out and down to the bed.

I frown at it. Who's leaving me notes?

But when I read it with sleep-gritty eyes, the words leave me cold, and an old, familiar sickness eats at my stomach.

Hands shaking, I look around my room as if a ghost might step out from a darkened corner.

The church hands these bookmarks out like candy, and it could have easily gotten pushed into my purse. And yet, as innocuous as it is, the words give me pause.

I don't know how long I stare at it. The cries from my dreams have faded in my ears, and my eyes have adjusted to the light pouring in the window. My stomach churns as I grab a book of matches.

I ignore my ringing phone as I drop the note in my bathroom sink.

The answering machine clicks on, then my mother's voice says, "Maggie." She sighs audibly. "Krystal said you showed up at the gallery yesterday. I'm sorry we didn't tell you, sweetie. We just weren't sure how. I hope you understand that she never wanted to hurt you."

I squeeze my eyes shut in frustration, wishing for blackness and oblivion. I want to forget. Will. Krystal. The last year. The sound of my father's voice in my head, as if he rose from the dead to leave that reminder in my purse. I want to forget the words typed so neatly on the church bookmark. The words that make me want to crawl out of my own skin.

I light a match and throw it into the sink, watch the words that have been ground into my brain since birth flame and turn them to ash.

Confess your sins and be forgiven.

"I'll have a twenty-ounce Guinness," I tell the scruffy middle-aged man behind the bar. My day started off like shit and didn't get much better. I made myself go to campus to re-enroll and discovered I lost my scholarship by dropping out last year. But, hey, my consolation prize is that they have an art studio available. That almost makes up for the thirty grand a year I'll be paying in tuition to finish my degree.

Brady turns his best glare on me and props his hands on his hips. "You still hell bent on making me lose my liquor license, girl?"

I offer him my ID from between two fingers. "I am legal now, old man. You can't kick me out anymore."

Brady examines the card with a furrowed brow. I handed him enough fake ones over the years, I can hardly be insulted by his skepticism. Before coming back home a month ago, I'd never legally had a drink in New Hope—not that I hadn't had my share of alcohol, mind you, just not legally.

Brady grunts and hands back my ID. "I guess I woulda known if I'd done the math." He shakes his head and draws me a beer.

I take a slow sip and scan the bar. My sisters were busy tonight—Lizzy with a date and Hanna with some sort of summer research gig for school—but I couldn't face my empty little rental tonight, couldn't handle the bare walls or the silence. After feeding Lucy, I decided to check out what it was like to be a patron at Brady's without having to dodge the proprietor.

Sadly, it's a little disappointing. It's a Thursday night, and apparently Brady's doesn't cater to a large, thirsty Thursday crowd in the summers. The place is nearly abandoned, save a couple guys in baseball caps playing a game of pool and a couple speaking in soft tones at the bar.

I'm bemoaning the silence when the screen at the front bangs shut and someone calls, "Lucy!"

I don't even flinch at that damn nickname anymore. I became numb to it when half my high school started using it—some behind my back, others to my face. In fact, I decided to reclaim it when I adopted my dog and bestowed the name upon her. Me and Lucy against the world.

Nevertheless, I turn around to see what asshole I have the pleasure of meeting tonight.

"I think you've got the wrong bar, sweet thang," Kenny Riles says, running his eyes over me and leaving a trail of slime behind. "The strip club is down the road."

"Fuck off, Kenny," I mutter.

I went to high school with this asshole and when shit hit the fan my freshman year, everyone was cruel, but Kenny and his buddies were the worst. And they never seemed to let it go.

He sidles up to me. Too close. I can smell his aftershave, a smell that might be pleasant if it weren't for its host. "When you were fifteen, I didn't get it. I didn't understand why a man would risk it all just to fuck you. But now…" His lips curl into a meaningful smirk as he trails off.

I feel sick.

The guys at the back table call to him, and he gives me a final once-over and winks before walking away.

My hands shake as I reach for my beer. I want to leave. I want to get as far away from here as possible, but I won't let him have that power over me. Instead, I settle into a stool at the bar and order something stronger.

chapter six

Asher

KNOW ANY hot men who can meet me down at Brady's and take my mind off a shitty day?

She summoned me with a simple text message. I programmed my number into her phone last week during our date—or, rather, our not-a-date—and I'd been beginning to wonder whether she'd ever use it.

The woman has driven me to distraction. Her laugh, her mind, that shield of indifference she hides behind. I keep thinking of the wicked look in her eyes as she stripped in front of me. My lust, the hungry desire to take her, hasn't faded. If anything, it's grown more intense.

Then there was the look on her face when that asshole called her *loose*. The flash of hurt, a wounded girl resurfacing for a split second before she pushed her away again. Physical attraction is something I can ignore. But this need to protect her from the pickup-driving assholes of the world? This need to uncover the woman hiding behind those walls? I'm consumed by it.

I walk into the bar and instantly spot her. That fiery red hair. Those wide green eyes. That smile that eats up her face.

Tonight she's wearing a little black number and knee-high heeled boots she had to have chosen for the express purpose of making me lose my mind.

There's an exposed strip of freckled skin between where the boots end and the skirt begins—two inches of soft flesh that make me want to drag her to the nearest closet and press her against the wall, slide into her hot, fast and hungry, her skirt bunched at her waist, her mouth hot against my neck.

Those two inches of skin are enough to make me forget that she's still hung up on some other guy.

Her lips tilt into a grin as she crosses to me, a little unsteady on her feet. "You came."

"You're drunk." The words come out with an unintended sigh.

She hooks her fingers into my belt loops and tugs me against her. "Not quite drunk. Not quite sober. Wanna take me home and take advantage of me?"

"Not if you're drunk," I say against her mouth. She smells so damn good, and I want to taste her, to touch her. I want to kiss my way down her body and find her sweet spots.

The tables in the front of the bar are empty and some guys sit at a booth at the back. "Who are you here with?" I ask.

"You now," she whispers.

"You're here drinking alone? You didn't bring a girlfriend to keep you company? To watch your back?"

She shakes her head and loops her arms around my neck. "I don't have girlfriends. Girls don't like me."

I'm sure this isn't something she'd share sober, so I let it drop. "How was your day?"

She leans her head against my chest. "Do you know what it feels like to have someone take away something you desperately wanted?"

Something jagged pushes down my throat at those words, but I don't reply. This isn't about me.

The jukebox thumps with a rock song and she rocks her hips against me to the beat, trailing a finger down the side of my face. "It's like she stole it from me, but I'm not allowed to think that because I'm the one who left him."

I'm not sure what she's talking about but I'm not about to interrupt. Apparently, Drunk Maggie is less averse to sharing.

"It was supposed to be our gallery," she whispers. "It was our dream but she took my spot. She stole my happily-ever-after."

"Your sister," I say, but she doesn't seem to hear me. She's rubbing against me like a cat, lost in her own pity party and the rhythm of the music.

"Girls like me don't get happily ever after." Her lips curl into a wicked smile that looks maniacal under such sad eyes. "Instead, the prince marries the good girl, and girls like me get to fuck him behind his wife's back. Lucky us."

"Jesus." I pull her into my arms and she burrows her head against my chest.

We dance, rolling our hips to the music, her body pressing closer and closer to mine. She's slipped a hand up my shirt. It's pressed between our bodies and her fingers are splayed against the hot skin of my abdomen. I like her here. Against me, curled into me like she might let me protect her.

She looks up at me with those big green eyes and seems to remember herself. She stutters back a step, pulling her hand from my shirt. "I need another drink," she says softly.

I grab her hand before she can go too far. "Don't. Please?" I draw her back to me and she tilts her chin up to look into my eyes.

"Why are you here, Asher?"

"You sent me a text inviting me, remember?"

She cocks her head. "But you won't have sex with me."

"Not tonight."

She crooks her finger and I lean down until her lips brush my ear. "But I want you. You won't regret it."

I straighten and look past her shoulder. "I will if you're thinking about *him* the whole time."

She spins around and spots Will and her sister. She backs into me, consciously or not, I'm not sure, but I wrap my arms around her, just under her breasts, and she settles her hands over mine.

"Maggie!" her sister calls, looking me up and down. "We were just talking about you." Krystal slides her hand into Will's and Maggie's hands squeeze mine.

Will's jaw ticks with tension, and when he looks me over, there's no hiding that he's sizing me up. But if I'm the competition, why is he marrying Krystal?

"Maggie's going to take an internship at our art gallery," Krystal is telling me.

"I haven't accepted yet," Maggie says stonily. Gone is her softness from earlier. She's put up her walls, sobered by the sight of this man.

"Consider it, Maggie," Will says. "Krystal's right. You're a perfect fit. You should be a part of it."

"Asher and I were just leaving." She turns toward the door, pulling me behind her.

I nod my goodbye and follow without question.

The door clatters behind us as we cross the gravel lot to her Mustang.

"Are you going to tell me what's between you and him?" I ask when we're alone.

"Not yet," she says softly, her voice and eyes more sober than they've been all night.

"I'm going to keep asking."

"I know." We lean side by side against her Mustang, and her answer is enough—for now. We let the sticky Indiana humidity lick at us, and she slides her hand into mine as we stare up at the country stars.

"When I was a little girl," she says softly, "my sisters and I would sneak out in the middle of the night and walk down to the river. We weren't allowed to be down by the water without an adult, but we didn't care. We'd lie on a blanket, just counting stars until we fell asleep."

I could imagine her there now, sitting on the riverbank after dark and watching the moonlight play off the water.

Sorrow creeps into those normally sharp eyes. She's kneading the corner of her lip between her teeth, and I want to dig deeper, but I know she'd tense her shoulders, put up that wall that says *Do Not Get Personal!* I don't want her to shut me out tonight, so I turn to her and put my hands against the car, pinning her in.

Her eyes change in an instant. The sorrow fades, swallowed up into that part of her that holds the rest of her secrets. Just as quickly, awareness flashes in its place. Her eyes turn hot.

I want her. Want to hold her. Want to feel her. Want to get inside and see what she is so desperate to protect. And I know the last is what she'll resist the most, but I'll start here.

I drop my lips to hers, and she lets me taste her.

I start with small kisses at the corners of her mouth until she relaxes beneath me, and her arms settle around my neck.

She tastes like beer. Beer and heat and that wildly addictive, odorless, tasteless drug that is Maggie.

Her tongue strokes mine. She sucks it into her mouth until my cock strains painfully against my fly.

I pull back and let my lips hover over hers.

"You could take me home," she whispers. "And leave me all hot and bothered again."

"I could."

"Or you could finish what we started in the pool."

I groan, pressing against her, my hands finding her waist, her hips, her ass. Nipping at her neck, sucking. I don't just want her, I need her. I need this. For reasons bigger than months of abstinence.

Maggie arches into me then tilts her head to give me better access to her neck. I sweep my tongue over that sweet juncture of her neck and shoulder and she shudders in my arms. I want to make her shudder in my bed. Suddenly I'm struck by an image of her bound and blindfolded. Vulnerable. Trusting. Open. *Mine.*

"I need to get you naked," I growl.

"Naked?"

"Or in that scrap of lace you wore when you did your striptease for me."

"I thought you weren't going to have sex with me."

I suck her earlobe into my mouth and tug it with my teeth. "We can get naked without having sex."

"I think you're doing it wrong." She licks her lips, eyes hot. "But you might convince me to try. As long as you don't mind spectators."

I groan into her neck. "Get into your car before I take you up on that."

I open the passenger door, and her keys jingle as she hands them over with a satisfied smile.

It takes about two minutes to get from Brady's to her house, but it feels like an eternity. She doesn't touch me, but tucks her finger in my belt loop like she's afraid I might sneak away. The air between us pulses thick and hot with sexual tension and anticipation.

When I pull into her driveway, I cut the engine and pull her against me. I kiss her, taste her, my fingers tangling in her hair.

Her hands snake up my shirt and she nips at my mouth with her teeth.

When I break the kiss, we're both breathing heavily.

She shoves lightly at my shoulders. "Inside, Exhibitionist Boy."

I grin and climb out of the car. Her hips sway as she leads the way into her house. My hands itch with the need to get her bare, to squeeze her ass as I taste her, to scrape my teeth over the flesh at her hips.

When Maggie opens the door, Lucy races toward her in big, bounding leaps. Then she spots me and immediately turns, tucks her nub of a tail, and runs for cover.

"Batting zero with the kid today." Maggie laughs as she heads to the back door. "Luce!" she calls, opening the screen. "Let's go outside."

The dog skitters past me with a pathetic combination whimper/bark/howl and runs for the door.

When Maggie turns back to me, her eyes are hot as they trail over my body. "Strip."

"Have you ever even *tried* letting someone else take the lead?"

She saunters across the kitchen and plucks at the buttons of my shirt. "What fun would that be?" Halfway down she abandons her task and pushes it off my shoulders, pressing open-mouthed kisses to my abdomen.

I reach for her dress, and she pushes my hands away and presses them against the counter.

"Oh no you don't," she warns. "Keep those hands right there."

I know she needs this—to take, to be in control—so I obey.

Her fingers finish their work on my shirt as her mouth explores—sucking, nibbling, making me lose my fucking mind.

"Mag—"

"Hush." Her hands work the button of my jeans.

I want to protest. Want to touch her, to watch the pleasure on her face as I taste her, but suddenly I'm against the counter, my shirt hanging from my wrists, my jeans around my thighs as Maggie drops to her knees. Her skirt hikes up her hips and exposes the tops of her soft thighs.

She cups me through my boxer briefs.

"Jesus," I gasp. I reach for her but she backs away.

"My house, my rules."

I'm lost as she frees my dick from my boxers. I want to be tender with this woman the world has battered, but I'm helpless as she strokes me with those soft hands. My hands itch to dive into her hair. To touch her breasts. To dip into her and make her scream. But I clasp the edge of the counter.

"I want to put you in my mouth." She's breathing hard, chest rising and falling, my cock a breath from her lips, wrapped up in her hand. "Are you safe?"

"Safe?" I swallow hard as she strokes me again, try to blink away the haze and translate words into meanings.

"I can get a condom for this part."

I tighten my grip on the counter. Because I don't deserve the woman on her knees, offering to suck latex to get me off. "Safe," I manage. "I haven't been with anyone without protection for over—"

I'm cut off by my own moan as she takes me into her mouth, gently laving the underside of my cock with her tongue. Her mouth closes around me, and I'm swallowed up by the wet, by the heat.

I won't close my eyes. I wouldn't miss the sight of her swollen lips around my cock. She pulls me deep and moans softly as her mouth contracts around my shaft. She draws back and returns, draws back. I fight the instinct to rock my hips but she curls her fingers into my thighs as she opens for me, her lips nearly to the base of my shaft.

"Maggie." I can't let it end like this. God, not tonight. Not yet. "Maggie."

I draw her up to me and kiss her.

Her lips are red and swollen from taking me. I want to remember her like this, want to stop for a minute and memorize the lust in her eyes and the flush of her cheeks. I'm ravenous for her and need to back off a little, to slow down, but she pulls me closer and strokes me between our bodies, and I'm drowning in need.

"Let me touch you," I whisper.

"Fuck me."

"No." I slide my hand between her thighs where I can feel her slick and swollen even through the thin lace of her panties. I squat before her, kissing my way down her thin cotton dress as I lower myself and her panties in a single motion. I pull them off over her boots and slide them from one foot at a time.

She tugs at my hair, drawing me up. "*Please, Asher.*"

I have to kiss her. I have to taste those lips again. I press her against the refrigerator, pictures and take-out menus flying. We're just limbs and heat and desire. She clings to me as I rock my hand between her thighs. She draws one leg up and wraps it around my waist as I slide a finger inside her, watching her face, reveling in her slick heat.

"You're so damn hot, so damn sweet."

Her hands tug lightly at my hair, and she makes little sounds at the back of her throat. I don't need to hear her cry of *Please* to know she wants more, but I resist the need to fuck, to claim, to bury myself in her.

She's a dream to watch. Masses of red hair, flashes of green eyes as she rolls her hips and loses herself in the pleasure I bring with my hand. I want her to break, to let go, but she's clinging to control.

I lower my mouth to her ear. "I don't fuck women who belong to someone else."

"I don't belong to anyone."

When I find her clit with my thumb, swollen and needy, she arches into me hard and her pussy squeezes me so damn beautifully as she pulses tight in orgasm.

Twenty thuds of my heart later, I come to my senses. Here's this woman in my arms I was so determined to treat gently. Her skirt's bunched around her waist, and bite marks swell at her neck.

Maybe it's seeing that red head pressed against my chest. Maybe it's the feel of her in my arms. Or maybe I hadn't wanted to remember before now.

But as I stand here, dizzy with arousal, I remember where I saw her before.

New Hope. The river. Jesus. How had I not put it together when I first looked into those big green eyes? I couldn't place them, and I've seen so many faces in my life, they all start to blend together.

Now the words slip out of my mouth before I can stop them. "God, Maggie. I'm so sorry."

Maggie

He is being ridiculous. One second I'm coming my brains out, his hot body pressed against my front, the cold refrigerator pressed against my back, the next he's apologizing to me? We were just about to have what I'm sure would have been off-the-charts hot kitchen sex, and then Mr. Nice Guy had to go and ruin my fun by apologizing. He's turning out to be one piss-poor excuse for a bad boy.

He sits at my kitchen table now, eyeing me. "Has anyone ever told you that you're moody?"

He's probably referring to the fact that I've been stomping around the house since that stupid S-word came out of his mouth and tarnished my after glow.

I grab two beers from the fridge and shove one in his hand. "You're *sorry*? How can you be sorry?"

He's pulled his pants back on, slid his arms back into his shirt—though it is still unbuttoned. We should be closing the deal. Maybe for a second time by now. In the bedroom, on the couch, in the shower. But instead I'm trying to figure out what the hell he thinks he needs to apologize for.

He narrows his eyes at me. "Because I had you up against the fridge with your dress hiked up around your waist. Because I didn't even take my goddamned shoes off, because whether you believe it or not, you deserve more than that."

I groan, running a hand through my hair and flopping into a kitchen chair. What am I thinking, getting involved with this man? He is too touchy-feely for me. "Asher, wake up and smell the third-wave feminism. Women have fantasies too. I happen to find a little frantic, half-clothed kitchen sex hot."

That makes him smile. "Me too." Then he ruins it by sighing and getting all serious again. "Listen. We need to talk."

I lean back in my chair. I'm not trying to get away from him exactly, but I'm never anxious to be closer to a man uttering those words. "You're not going to ruin this by declaring your eternal love for me, are you?" I take a pull from my beer, noticing he hasn't touched his. "Because, damn it, Asher, I thought better of you."

He averts his gaze, making me feel a little panicky until he says, "I do know you from somewhere."

"Wait. What?"

"I know you from somewhere."

"That wasn't just a line after all?" My laughter dies on my lips when I see the gravity in his eyes.

"We met twelve months ago."

I feel myself pale, the blood draining from my face and gathering low in my belly where it roils. I push away from the table.

Granny was right. My past really is returning. Because twelve months ago, my world changed.

chapter seven

Asher

"I WAS going to name her Grace."

When I first saw the girl sitting by the river twelve months ago, there was so much blood on her hands, I worried she had slit her wrists.

"Miss?" The redhead sat on the bank of the river, knees drawn to her chin. She ignored me and stared at her bloodstained hands like a tragic Shakespearean tableau.

"Are you okay?" I inched closer and saw a smudge of blood under her eye, streaked where the tears had run through it. I couldn't get a good look at her wrists, but assumed she had cut herself there, come to my little edge of river to let the life bleed out of her. "Where are you hurt?"

She blinked at me, seeming to register my presence for the first time. God. She was probably doped up on all sorts of drugs.

She shook her head frantically. "I'm not hurt. I'm fine. It's just a little blood. This happens to some women."

But then she squeezed her eyes shut, clung to her legs, and rocked herself back and forth.

"What's your name?" I kept my voice low, gentle, as I inched closer.

"I was going to name her Grace," she whispered, eyes focused on the river as if it could save her.

"Who?"

She bit her lip, shook her head. "I didn't want this. Not this."

She reached a hand down, cupped herself between her legs as if she were trying to hold something there.

I understood then. I lowered myself on the ground next to her, felt the dampness of the riverbank seep into my pants. "You're having a miscarriage?"

She shook her head again. "I was going to make it work. It wasn't ideal, maybe not right, but I was going to make it work. I didn't want this. This can't be happening."

"You need to go to the hospital."

Her eyes grew wide, and I was struck by how her irises were a solid jade green. "Would you go with me? I don't think I can be alone when they tell me I'm losing my baby. I"—she gasped for air, choked on a sob—"I'm so afraid."

And then I surprised us both by pulling her into my arms and holding her while she cried.

I never forgot the way all concern seemed to leech out of her as we approached the hospital. I never forgot the way her voice changed, became monotone, as if, so young, she'd already lost all faith in life. I hadn't been able to forget her haunted expression as I parked in the hospital's circle drive and she'd watched the sliding doors that lead to the ER. *Do you believe God punishes us for our sins?*

I thought about her after that day. I wondered what had happened after the nurses took her back. I waited two hours, smudges of a strange woman's blood on my shirt.

How could the Maggie who keeps a steel cage around her heart be the same woman who cupped herself between her legs to keep her baby inside?

Maggie

There's so much pity in Asher's eyes, I can't stand it.

"I didn't realize," he says. "I couldn't figure out how I knew you. You look so different now. Healthier than you did then. Your hair's different, maybe? I only knew what you looked like when you were crying. I found you by the river. Took you to the hospital."

Asher Logan was the stranger who took me in that day? Is the world really that small? Is fate really so cruel?

I was such a complete wreck that day at the river. I remember a man. Remember him trying to get me to go to the hospital.

I stare at my hands, almost surprised to see them clean. No blood, no horrible nightmare making me face my sins.

How can this all be coming back? But then, I never escaped it, did I?

"You held me."

"Yeah," he whispers, "I did."

I was praying by the river that day. Confused. Guilty. Mixed up as hell. I was pregnant, and I was getting married in two days, and I had no idea when my life had gotten so completely out of control.

Then, when I started bleeding, it was like some sick answer to my prayer. *Dear God, please make this right.* And then blood.

I don't hear Asher move, but when I look up, when I take my eyes off my unstained hands, he is standing next to me, extending a hand.

I could take it. No doubt, he'd hold me again. No doubt, it would feel damn good. He'd stroke my hair, murmur in my ear. He'd listen to me blubber like an idiot woman who can't deal with a traumatic situation—or even the memory of one—without the strong arms of a man to hold her together.

I'm tempted. I'm truly tempted, and I hate myself for that. Even twelve months later. Even after therapy and endless affirmations of self-forgiveness, I'm tempted. I want to tell someone. I want to start at the beginning. I want to start with my father. With being fifteen and seeing the word CONFESS appear like a phantom in the steam of the bathroom mirror. I want to spill my ugly soul out onto the cold, scarred linoleum of the kitchen floor.

At least then I wouldn't need to worry about any unwanted declarations of love—because then he would know just how damaged I am.

Asher reaches for me, but I ignore his hand. I wrap my arms across my chest because I won't let myself need his.

"I'm sorry you had to see me that way," I say. I need to get away from him. Away from the reminder. Coming back to New Hope is hard enough with all these pieces of my past returning, threatening to stir up questions I can't answer. This month—the anniversary of Asher pulling me from the riverbank and taking me to the hospital, the anniversary of the cancellation of my sham of a wedding, the anniversary of making the hardest decision I've ever made in my life—this month is the hardest yet. And my life has been no day at the fair.

"I hope you'll respect my privacy and keep that day between the two of us."

To Asher's credit, he doesn't come to me but neither does he retreat. He holds his ground, stands solid. "Of course."

I nod, and I'm so confident I can trust him that I want to weep. "Listen, it's been fun, but I think you should go. Do you need a ride back to your car?"

"No. I can walk." He doesn't move for a long moment, and I wonder if he'll argue. I wonder if he's having fantasies of holding the pieces of me together while I sleep. Will's words haunt me.

"Maggie, if you're broken, I'll fix you."

I won't be the woman who needs that from a man. I won't.

Asher is staring at me—waiting for something—but I can't meet his eyes.

I wait until I hear the clang of the front door.

I run the water hot at the kitchen sink. While squirting liquid soap on my hands, I think of the bookmark I found in my purse. *Confess your sins and be forgiven.*

My sins? I don't even know where to start.

I raise the mallet and hesitate a single heartbeat before bringing it down on the glossy purple serving tray. The sound of cracking ceramic lifts that ever-present weight from my shoulders, and I slam the hammer down a second time, and a third, until there's no platter, only purple shards that send my right brain spinning.

Next I have an aquamarine vase I found at a thrift shop. I can't wait to shatter it. And the mugs from the Salvation Army, and the ceramic tiles from my mom's bathroom renovation.

This is my new obsession. Mosaics. I came to Sinclair on a scholarship for painting, and I know how my professors are going to react to my new medium when I return in the fall. Ethan Bauer will call it a waste of my talent. Mosaics aren't *real* Art, he'll say, not the kind with the capital *A*. They're backyard tinkering. They're the layman's work. They're— Ethan's biggest insult to an artist—a *craft*.

But I think that's why I've fallen in love with them. I like finding beauty in these discarded treasures. I like making something where there was nothing before.

Being back on campus feels odd. A little like returning to a former life after being reincarnated. Being in this studio gives me a sense of *déjà vu*.

I take another sip of cranberry juice and smile at the rising sun peaking in the window of my art studio. Getting studio space means getting a key to the fine arts building, and after Asher left last night, I grabbed my keys and headed to campus. The only stop I made was for a bottle of cranberry juice and a bottle of vodka.

And if I'm a little drunk at seven in the morning, who am I hurting?

I'm unsteady on my feet—from the liquor and the exhaustion—and I have to balance myself with a hand against the table.

Glass pops, snapping under my palm. I see blood before I even register the pain. A little blood smeared across the bubbled glass, then a lot of blood. Then the pain—dull and throbbing as red liquid puddles on the floor.

I put my hand to my mouth. My fingers tighten around the wound. I'm okay. Maybe I need a few stitches, but I'll be all right.

But then I look at my hands. Really look. And the sight of them covered in blood sends me back to the river. Back to the day I thought I was losing my baby. Suddenly, breathing is too difficult. The air is too thick and the path to my lungs too narrow.

Then I'm crying. My tears are hitting the floor, mixing with the bright red blood.

I have to get to the bathroom. Wash this up. But I'm stuck in the past. My feet and my brain, frozen in time.

I don't know how long I stand there before Will shows up at my door.

"Maggie!" He rushes in and grabs my hands. And now the blood's on his hands too and that's not right. He's innocent in this. He doesn't deserve to be stained by my mistakes.

He's murmuring something and I realize he's wrapping up my hand in some sort of cotton. Where did he...

His shirt. He's torn off his shirt and is wrapping the gash in my hand in the soft cotton. Damn, that's sweet. And now he's standing in front of me in nothing but his jeans. I'm bleeding through his makeshift bandage, but I can't take my eyes off his chest.

"You're so gorgeous." Did I say that out loud? I didn't mean to. But he is. Will pushes his body hard—long runs and strict appointments with the weights. I always laughed at how regimented he was with his fitness, but now I'm thinking the world would be a better place if more men were so dedicated. There would be more happiness. Less war. Fewer children would go hungry.

I hear myself giggling and I'm looking into Will's face. He's taken my face into his hands and is saying...something.

Were his lips always so perfect?

"Maggie." He gives me a soft shake.

They were always that perfect. I remember. I remember wishing I were a different kind of girl so I could kiss those lips without feeling like I was tarnishing something so beautiful. "I'm sorry. What?"

"I'm taking you to the hospital."

I smile. "You're going to take care of me? Don't you just want me to bleed out? Wouldn't that be...easier?" Then I laugh because I sound so damn dramatic.

He frowns, says something about shock. Then he leans so close to my face I think he's going to kiss me. I tilt my lips up and wait. I miss the feel of his mouth on mine.

He draws in a deep breath through his nose. "You're drunk."

I lift a shoulder. "I'm legal now."

"Jesus," he mutters. He's saying something else, looking around my studio for something, but I can't take my eyes off his gorgeous bare skin, the expanse of his back. Did I kiss him there when I had the chance? Why can't I remember?

He grabs my purse and wraps his arm around my waist. The next thing I know, we're on the elevator, and I'm leaning into him. He's so warm.

"Yeah, and you're drunk," he says.

I frown. Did I say something?

Then we're walking again and he's settling me into the car, and I think I might have fallen asleep a little because now he's opening my door and pulling me to my feet. He has a shirt on again. When did that happen? Why did it happen?

"Why are you being so nice to me?" I ask.

"I'm not being nice. You're just too drunk to notice I'm pissed at you."

His arm is wrapped around my waist, and we're moving through sliding doors. He says something to the man sitting behind the counter, while I blink, my eyes objecting to the fluorescent lights.

"You're mad at me?"

He settles me into a chair and inspects my hand. The cotton is soaked through with bright red blood that doesn't look real at all. It looks like something out of a B-grade film.

"Do you often get trashed and play with sharp pieces of glass?"

Oh. I hear it now. He is pissed. I smile. I like when Will gets pissed. He's being all sweet and protective, and it makes me feel like I'm worth something more than the trash we all know I am. "I can't create art if I'm not relaxed," I object.

"It's stupid and it's dangerous." He settles into the seat next to me, and I lean my head on his shoulder. He's frowning at me, so I smile up at him. I've ruined his night. Then I laugh because it's not night anymore, and Will was probably starting his day. He probably had work to do. Department meetings. Curriculum development. I've ruined his day.

"You haven't ruined anything." His eyes meet mine and even twelve shades of tipsy, I can see the pain there, the confusion. His eyes stay locked on mine for so long, this should probably feel awkward. But this is Will and I've loved him forever. I could look at him forever. I could let him look at me forever. If I didn't believe he deserved better.

"That's you," he says.

I blink and realize they're calling my name.

Nodding, I only teeter a little as I push myself to standing.

I'm two steps toward the door before I realize he hasn't moved. I stop and turn to him. "Come with me?" I bite my lip, watching the battle play out across his face. I don't want to explain. The loneliness. This fear that it might swallow me whole and I'll just disappear. The bigger fear that everything might be easier if it did. "Please?"

He stands and wraps his arm around me, and as he leads me back to the examination room, I tell myself I'm only leaning into him because I'm drunk. I tell myself it's okay because I'm hurt. But the pleasure I feel at having his arm wrapped around me? The way his heat and low murmurs chase away the loneliness so much better than the vodka did?

I don't have an excuse for that.

William

She's drunk. She's drunk and she's hurt and she's in shock.

But that doesn't change the fact that I love the feel of her in my arms. I love having her *need* me like she does right now.

The doctor stitched up her wound, a gash that extended from the palm of her hand down into her wrist and required twelve stitches.

She's stitched and bandaged and now they want her to sober up before they'll release her.

"How'd you find me?" she asks. The alcohol is leaving her system. I can tell by the way she's pulling away, remembering herself.

"You were making enough noise to wake the dead. I just heard all this glass breaking, and then I heard you crying."

She blinks. "I wasn't crying."

I tuck her hair behind her ear. She still has streaks of blood on her cheeks. The doctor wanted to do a psych eval, but I talked her out of it, convinced her Maggie wasn't a threat to herself, but I'm not even sure I believe that. When I saw all that blood…

Her eyes are on my mouth, and her lips are parted just so. "You saved me."

"You would have sobered up enough to get yourself to the hospital eventually," I offer, more for myself than her, because this thing that has me holding her so tightly is the soul-scorching fear that she wouldn't have, that by the time she came to her senses she would have lost too much blood, and then it would have been too late.

She leans her head back, taking her eyes from me to focus on the ceiling—thank God. "You're always there when I need someone. You're always ready to save me."

"Not always," I say softly, and her eyes connect with mine so quickly, I'm sorry I said anything at all.

"That wasn't your fault."

I shrug. "I wasn't there." My gut twists at the memory. How many times can one man fail Maggie Thompson?

She gives me a sloppy grin. "Look, Will. I broke and you fixed me."

"Maggie." I remember that promise. It's a promise I'd keep today if she'd take me up on it. There's nothing I want more than to see her whole after years of walking around broken.

"Why didn't you hate me? After? Everyone else hated me, but you…"

I focus on her bandaged hand as the memory takes me back to fifteen-year-old Maggie showing up unannounced in my dorm room in Notre Dame, her eyes sad, though she promised she was fine; her hands greedy, though I wouldn't let her touch me. *Just don't make me go back there. I can't do it anymore. Let me stay. Please.* But I'd taken her to the bus station and sent her home. A month later, the town was overcome by the scandal. They blamed her, but I knew better because if she'd wanted any of it, she wouldn't have been in my dorm room begging me not to send her home.

I rest my hand over her bandaged palm. "I could never hate you, Maggie. Not when you were the pipsqueak neighbor girl and not when you were breaking my heart by leaving me."

She lifts her good hand to my face, her eyes on mine. "I was an idiot." Then she leans toward me and our lips brush.

Hot, electric arousal grips me. "Would you ask me to leave her?" I whisper against her lips. "Would you tell me if you still needed me?"

She flinches as if I've struck her. "I can't do that to her."

chapter eight

Maggie

LAST NIGHT, I dreamt of my father. His hurt, disappointed eyes stared back at me from behind my bathroom mirror, making me feel dirty in my own skin. Because of my own skin.

Then he was pushing me into church, but I wasn't the fifteen-year-old girl he'd shamed into confession. I was an adult. Blood stained my hands as I folded them in prayer and he whispered in my ear, *"Confess your sins and be forgiven."*

I woke to the sounds of a baby crying and jumped out of bed. I tripped over my feet as I scrambled toward the bassinet I don't own to comfort a baby I don't have.

Then I took a hot shower and scrubbed my skin until it was red and angry, and I dressed for church with my family. Operation New Me puts me in a church pew next to my mother at least once a month. Mom would prefer this happen weekly, but I've read that when you're committed to a change, you should set realistic goals.

I could have done without the sermon—a self-important speech about the decline in American family values as illustrated by teenage promiscuity, extra-marital affairs, abortion, and babies born out of wedlock. The priest nailed me with his condemning gaze again and again as he spoke. I don't have proof, but I'm pretty sure he planned this one for my return.

Asshole.

I sat through the whole sermon with Will's voice in my head. *"Would you ask me to leave her? Would you tell me if you still needed me?"*

I tried to tune out the priest by figuring out what Will had meant by that. Does that mean that he wants me or that he wants to protect me? Does he even know there's a difference? But I couldn't come to any conclusions with the priest warning the congregation against Jezebels and guilt surging up in my throat.

Mom always has Sunday brunch at her house after church, but the food isn't much to look forward to. As I study the buffet, my stomach growls in protest. Today's fare consists of fresh veggies and yogurt dip, fresh fruit, low-carb deli "sandwiches" wrapped in lettuce, and mimosas made with half-calorie orange juice. Mom is clearly on the warpath again, attempting to prove her worth as a human being by the size of her daughters' jeans.

Hanna is convinced this obsession is her fault and has apologized countless times for her "weight problem," resulting in bland family meals. Hanna's heavier than the rest of us, but she's gorgeous and wears it so well she's even been approached to be a plus-size model. Of course, that only embarrassed her, so she never pursued it.

"Hey," Hanna says with a slight bob of her head toward the door. "Don't look now, but I think Mrs. Bauer just came in."

"Claudia? Ethan's wife?" The words are out of my mouth before I realize the "Ethan's wife" part would have been better left unsaid.

"I personally think she's dense," Lizzy says. "What woman in her right mind would stay married to Professor Infidelity? You can't tell me she doesn't know."

I stiffen. "Know about what?"

"Oh, come on!" Lizzy turns her calculating gaze on me. "Everybody knows he sleeps with half his models. Be honest, haven't you fantasized a little about getting yourself a piece of delectable art professor ass?"

"Me?" I clutch my chest. "What the hell does that mean?"

"Come on, Maggie, every girl at Sinclair with a pulse and an inclination toward men is hot for Dr. Bauer. I saw the way you looked at him. Hell, it's the only time I've seen you go all gushy over a guy."

"I did not go *all gushy*. There's not a gushy bone in my body."

"There was with Dr. Bauer!" Lizzy sings.

"I'm an artist. I admire his work!" I'm quickly edging into *doth protest too much* territory, so I back down. "Anyway, I've grown up since then." And I have. Too bad I had to do it the hard way.

I fill my plate and take a seat between Hanna and Lizzy.

My youngest sister settles into a seat across from me, her plate heaping with fruit and low-carb sandwiches.

My mom clears her throat. "Portion control, Abby," she says softly.

"She's growing," I protest.

"I'm just trying to save her the heartache of being overweight."

Hanna winces beside me.

I push back from the table.

"Where are you going now, Maggie?"

"I need a cigarette." I say, though I find smoking repulsive.

I step onto the back deck and close my eyes. The sound of the river rushing beyond the backyard calms me as I sink onto the steps.

"Are you okay, Maggie?"

Claudia Bauer closes the door behind her as she joins me on the deck. Just the sight of her makes guilt settle over me. My mom seems to have taken Claudia under her wing, and since I've been home it seems like she's at the house as often as I am.

The woman has this classic, old-money kind of beauty. High cheekbones, delicately arched eyebrows, and a perfectly straight nose. Claudia keeps her hair bleached a platinum blond and cut just past her chin. Two-carat diamond stones sparkle at her ears.

Does Claudia know that her husband purchased those earrings for his mistress?

"I'm okay," I lie. I'm not okay. I don't want to be here, and I don't want to pretend to be the good daughter. I don't want to see my little sister grow up with the same unrealistic expectations I did, and I don't want to continue to dodge my past.

"No, you're not." Claudia lowers herself next to me. As an awkward teen, I always wished for the grace of women like Claudia. As a cocky college student, I finally accepted it wasn't in me.

Claudia sighs. "I always knew when you weren't okay, darling. You can fool everyone else, but I've got you figured out."

I turn to her. "Do you, now?" Though it's a possibility. Like her art professor husband Ethan, Claudia is an artist, and my mom sent me to her studio for lessons as a teen. She always looked out for me. Then, when I started at Sinclair and moved into a little rental house with Lizzy and Hanna, Claudia looked out for all of us.

I choose one hell of a way to return the favor.

My gut folds on itself under the weight of my self-loathing.

"Yes." Claudia's pink lined lips curve up in a smile. "You were always so tough. It never occurred to anyone that you might have some of those same college-girl insecurities as your sisters. I could always tell when you were upset. You'd storm into the studio worried about Hanna or on a mission to save Lizzy from flunking out when she'd been on another party binge."

"So, you're saying I was *always* upset?" I say, trying for humor.

"I'm saying"—Claudia twirls the cross at her neck—"that you don't fool people as well as you think you do." She smiles sweetly. "Now I'm going to go back inside. After you finish that cigarette of yours, I hope you join us."

"Thanks," I mutter, suddenly wishing I did smoke so I could delay my return.

When I join them, Claudia is chatting with my mother in the corner, and a small shiver runs from my toes all the way up my spine.

At fifteen, I fell from my father's grace. He would tell me I was a harlot sent by the devil to destroy men. He never said this to my sisters, never suspected they were anything but innocent. I was special in this way alone. Of course, I'd given him all the proof he needed.

Over the last year, I've wondered if he knew who I would become, what I would do. Or if I became what I am because his speeches were so damn convincing.

William

My always-beautiful fiancée is forever exfoliating and moisturizing and wrinkle-removing. I watch her as she rubs lotion onto her utterly perfect legs.

"I kissed her. I kissed Maggie. At the hospital."

Krystal freezes for one heartbeat. Two. Then she swallows so hard I can hear it before she resumes her task. "Is that all?"

"Krys, it was stupid. I was caught up in the past, so worried about her. I wasn't even thinking." I force myself to stop. There's no explanation that can make this *okay*. "I'm worried about her."

"Thank you for telling me," she says softly.

"Don't do this. Don't pretend it's no big deal. This matters, Krystal. I fucked up and it's not okay."

When she lifts her gaze to mine, her big brown eyes are so sad they make my chest ache. I wish she'd say something, anything. I wish she'd scream at me. At least then I'd know she still cares.

"Let's just leave town." I'm pacing the length of the bedroom. "We can open a gallery somewhere else. We can start a new life somewhere."

"You know we can't do that."

"We'll take Grandma with us. Some of her friends moved to a retirement community in Naples. We could take her there and find a place of our own." I squeeze her hands between both of mine. "You love the beach."

"What happened to wanting to raise your kids in New Hope?" she asks softly. "What happened to not wanting to uproot Grandma?"

I look at the floor. When Maggie wasn't around, I didn't doubt for a minute whether our love was strong enough. How do I explain that all changed the minute she came back to town? "I want this to work. You are so damn good for me."

Her hand touches my jaw, and the contact is so unexpected, so overdue, my nerves flair to life under her fingertips. "Do you love me, Will?"

"Yes." I want to lower my mouth to hers, to kiss her until we both forget everyone else, but I'm too afraid it wouldn't work.

"Do you still love her?"

The words wrap their fingers around my heart and squeeze painfully. "Don't ask me that."

She gives me a sad smile and pushes herself off the bed. "I'm going to bed," she says softly. "I'll see you in the morning."

"And then what? What happens next for us?"

She freezes, her back to me. "Do you think she was trying to commit suicide?" Krystal hugs herself and rubs her bare arms. The house is warm, but ever since I told her about finding Maggie this morning, she's been shivering.

"You can imagine why she might consider it, can't you? Even her own goddamned sister has taken to calling her *Lucy*. And you and me..." I trail off. Making Krystal feel guilty about Maggie's "accident" isn't productive, and with the tension between my fiancée and me right now, we need our conversations to be productive. Because this limbo is hell.

"When I called her that the other day, I was angry. Scared. It was the only time I've ever called her that." She bites down on her lower lip. "Do you really think the you and me part..."

I close my eyes. "Her accident wasn't your fault. She was drunk..." The truth is, I have no idea if Maggie's injury was a drunken accident or a botched suicide attempt.

Krystal shakes her head and watches the river run by on the other side of the glass. "She drinks too much." Her voice is heavy with worry.

"You can't save her."

In the mirror, I see her close her eyes. "Says the pot to the kettle," she murmurs softly. "I'm just so worried."

"Me too." I watch her leave the room, but I don't know if we're talking about Maggie or us.

At the other end of the house, I hear Krystal locking up for the night and then the soft thump of her bedroom door as she goes to bed. We don't sleep together. She doesn't want us to have sex until our wedding night. Well, our *next* wedding night. She's become more conservative in the last few years, more concerned about pleasing her mother or her church or her God. Maybe all three, I'm not sure. I just know it's important to her so I don't push the issue.

In fact, since Maggie's been home, it's been a bit of a relief. Krystal's right. I've changed. But so has she, and I can't imagine fucking her right now. And *making love* is out of the question. There's too much tension between us, and we can't snuggle close when we're both wound up so tightly in thorny vines of doubt.

I lie on top of the covers and turn off the light. I stare up at the ceiling in the darkness.

I'm not sure I can go through with this wedding. When that stink bomb went off, it was so surreal, and then everyone started running out of the church and I was just...*relieved.*

Krystal has been a constant in my life since we were kids. We went through school together and went to college together. We both decided to move home after graduating from Notre Dame.

She was always there. Always a friend. And when Maggie canceled the wedding and skipped town, Krystal was there to hold my hand.

Our relationship was so *normal,* and I found comfort in that normalcy. When Maggie didn't take my calls or return my emails, Krystal became a fixture in my life.

While Maggie always thought I was too good for her, Krystal had every confidence that she was good enough for *any* man.

I force myself to close my eyes, but my mind spins wildly with the implications of the decision I need to make. I love Krystal. I love that she believes in herself. I love that she believes in me. And Maggie? I don't even know if I love her. I crave her. I need her.

I want to stop waiting. I want to start living my life. Only one woman can do that with me. And only one wants to.

But as I wrap my hand around my dick, she's not the one I'm thinking of. Instead, my mind conjures the memory of a feisty redhead in my little apartment by campus. It's a go-to memory for me. I was finishing up my first semester of graduate classes at Sinclair and Maggie was a freshman.

She sat cross-legged on my couch, scanning the music collection on my phone while I pretended not to be mesmerized by her smile.

"How's the love life going?" she asked, suddenly bored with my phone and tossing it next to her on the couch.

From my spot on the floor, I ran my eyes over her face. Those big eyes, the sprinkle of freckles across the bridge of her nose that contrasted so sharply with her wicked smile. "There's not much of a love life to speak of."

She rolled her eyes. "You're a big, bad graduate student now. A TA. An ar*tist.* I see the girls swoon over you. Pick one."

I remember studying her, wondering if she really didn't know. "Maybe I already have."

"So, what's stopping you?" She slid off the couch and sat in front of me on the floor, taking my face in her hands. "You're amazing."

I wanted to lower my mouth to hers and kiss her, but I knew that would scare her off. I'd wanted to kiss her since she showed up in my dorm room at Notre Dame and asked me to. But at Notre Dame she was too young, and there in my New Hope apartment I was too afraid of losing her to make that move. So I said, "Maybe I doubt my skills."

She laughed. "What skills? Kissing?" When I didn't reply, she frowned. "Fucking?"

"No." My cheeks warmed. Maggie used sex as a shield, and as a result she could talk about it—any part of it—without batting a lash. "Why is it that some girls don't like oral sex?"

Maggie snorted. "Because having a cock shoved down your throat isn't all it's cracked up to be?" She lifted a shoulder, shrugging. "But then I can't really talk for them, I kind of like giving head. It's"—her gaze dropped to my pants then quickly returned to my face—"a power trip."

Oh, hell. The image of her mouth sliding over my cock slammed into me so fast and hard, I had to shift on the floor to ease my discomfort. "I'm not talking about that kind of oral sex."

Her eyes went big and she grinned. "Going down on *her*? That's what you're talking about? What girl doesn't like that?"

I shrug. "Some girls don't."

"Really? Why not?" She frowned. "Are you doing it right?"

I grunted. "Yeah, I'm pretty sure I know what's going on down there."

She lifted a brow. "You sure about that? Maybe you need a second opinion."

"Maggie, what are you doing?" My breath clogged in my chest because suddenly she was shifting on the floor, slipping her panties off from under her skirt. They were white cotton with little rainbows, and as she slid them down her legs, I wanted to touch her so badly my hands nearly burned with all the live-wire nerves. When she pulled them off and tossed them on the couch behind her, I thought I might suffocate from the weight of the desire in my chest.

"Where do you want me? The couch? The floor? Your bed?"

"I'm not just going to use your body like some sort of dummy I can practice on." But even then Maggie was my kryptonite.

When she lifted her face, her expression softened, and I was torn in two by what I saw in her eyes. First, I saw her old need to validate her worth with her body, the reason I refused to touch her when she came to my dorm as a fifteen-year-old. But there was more. I wouldn't have touched her if I hadn't seen it—the lust sparking in her eyes, the way her breathing grew uneven.

The air between us was tense with everything we never said, heavy with the knowledge that this was it for us because we were too different in one way: I loved her. And Maggie? She hated herself with such an intensity that no one she respected could get close.

And now, as my shaft pulses thick against my palm, Maggie fills my brain so completely, there's no room for the self-disgust I should be feeling. In this moment, hanging in the web of the memory, there's no room for guilt. I let myself remember the way she looked as she sat on the edge of the couch and parted her legs, my veins zipping with the forbidden heat of putting my mouth on a woman I'd never even kissed. I let myself remember the first brush of my lips against her inner thigh and the shudder that went through her. Finally, I let myself remember the feel of her against my lips, the taste of her on my tongue, and the sound of her moans as I loved her in the only way she would let me.

As my cock grows slick, the memory moves forward sixteen months in time, her hair spread out around her on the wet grass by the river, her face framed by my hands as I dipped my head for a kiss so long-anticipated that it's the most erotic thing my mind can conjure in this moment, as I tighten my grip and push myself into release.

After, the self-loathing settles in, as it should. I stare up at the ceiling, hating everyone who ever made me believe that love was simple, that it was easy.

If love were simple, my love for Krystal would be enough to wash away the memory of Maggie's kiss.

Maggie

This new bridesmaid dress is more hideous than the first.

"What do you think?" Hanna asks as I step from the dressing room.

"It's…" *Hideous.* I search for another word. "So unique!"

"We hate it too," Hanna whispers.

I frown. I don't *hate* it, not exactly. It seems cruel to hate such an ugly dress. Akin to hating an ugly child.

The first strike against the dress is its color: maize, a fancy way of saying "sweet-corn yellow." The hue washes me out and makes me look a little malnourished.

The second strike against the dress is the skirt. The base is tea length. I can go for tea length. I even thought the skirt looked cute landing just below my knees. But it has a removable floor-length skirt that wraps around three-quarters of the dress, exposing only a small triangle of the shorter skirt beneath.

The third, and biggest, strike against the dress is the big ass bow sitting right at my hip.

No, I don't hate the dress. I just find it to be a little schizophrenic. Sexy casual here, formal there, little-girl cute there. The combination is disturbing.

Krystal flounces into the dressing room and pretends I don't exist. "Aren't they the best?" she asks Hanna and Lizzy, looking them over. "You are the loveliest BMs ever!" And with that, she leaves the room, calling for the bridal shop's dressing room attendant.

I bite my lip. *BMs?*

"I've been called a lot of things…" Lizzy mutters.

"She's spending too much time on online wedding planning forums," Hanna explains. Then she drops her voice to a whisper. "You'd think she wanted us to look ugly."

Not sure what else to do, I turn to study my dress in the mirror. Goddamn it's ugly. This is a dress that needs someone to take pity on it and put it out of its misery. Bridesmaid dress euthanasia should be a thing.

"Maybe it's just missing something," I try.

"Yeah," Lizzy agrees. "Like a brown paper bag."

The dressing room attendant returns without Krystal. She's wringing her hands and cringing. "Um, I think your sister needs you."

That's when I hear it. Ever so faintly, I hear the hiccoughing sobs of my big sister in her dressing room.

Hanna, Lizzy, and I exchange worried glances before turning toward the door. I think about staying away, I think about letting the twins comfort her, but there was a Maggie-and-Krystal long before there was a Maggie-and-Will, and right now she needs her sisters. All of us.

My breath catches in my throat as I step into her dressing room. Krystal looks drop-dead gorgeous in white. Her long dark hair contrasts sharply against the fabric and makes her look exotic. Not to mention the things the corseted waist and low-cut neckline do for her cleavage. Even collapsed into a pool of white satin, she's beautiful.

And she's crying like I've never seen her cry before.

"I want to talk to Maggie."

Lizzy and Hanna look at each other and then at me.

I nod, letting them know it's okay. When they're gone, I close the door to give us some privacy. "Krys?"

She sniffs and peers up at me through her lashes. "Do you hate me?"

"No," I say, but the word breaks, catching on something in my throat. "I could never hate you, Krys."

"You should."

I sink down onto the floor next to her, careful not to snag my dress. "I left *him*," I say softly.

I wonder again if Will ever told her the truth about our wedding—what little of the truth he knew, that is.

Krystal's shoulders tremble with her inhale. "You were too young."

"I was," I agree.

"We all knew you were terrified of getting married. It was right there in your eyes every time we brought it up. You didn't run away from Will. You ran away from marriage." She sniffs and wipes her cheek with the back of her hand. "And I swooped in and took him before you had a chance to come back to him."

I look at my hands. How can I deny what she's saying when I've thought the exact same thing?

"I told myself I didn't care what you thought," she says. "I told myself you could hate me if you wanted, but I deserved to marry the man I love. But I was lying to myself."

"It doesn't matter. He's in love with you now. You're in love with him. Nothing else matters."

"We both know that's bullshit. We both know love is never enough."

Her hand is tucked into the pools of satin around her. I find it and slide my fingers through hers. "It is if you let it be."

She lifts her head to look at me. Tears have clotted in her lashes, and there's a faint line of mascara down each cheek. "I'm sorry, Maggie."

"I'm okay," I whisper. Even if it's not true just yet, there's something blossoming inside me that believes some day it might be.

"No marriage is worth losing you. No man is worth that."

"You aren't going to lose me, Krys. I came home, remember?"

Her eyes leave my face and settle on our joined hands. She turns mine over and runs her fingers over the gauze at my wrist.

I snatch my hand away. "That was an accident."

Her brows draw together. "You'd tell me, wouldn't you? If you just couldn't handle me and Will, you'd tell me?"

I take her face in my hands and wipe away her tears. "Of course," I promise, but I don't know if the lie is for her sake or mine.

chapter nine

Maggie

I HAVEN'T been back to my studio since the accident, and I expect to find a bloody mess waiting for me, but someone's been here in front of me. I know, without asking, that it was Will. He wouldn't have wanted everyone else to see it, wouldn't have wanted me to have to endure the questions.

I don't let myself think about last Friday morning at all. Instead, I dive into my work. Or attempt to. With my left hand immobilized, there's not much I can do but bust up some more glass.

There's a knock outside my office, and I bring the mallet down one last time before I answer it—leaving crystal shards behind as I cross the tiny room.

When I open the door, I'm surprised to see Asher standing on the other side, hands tucked in his pockets, eyebrow quirked. He's wearing jeans and a fitted gray t-shirt that pulls across his chest. Tattoos peek out from where the sleeves strain around his biceps, and I want to take a bite of him he looks so delicious.

"Sounds like a herd of elephants in a china shop in there," he says.

"Something like that." I cross my arms. He should probably be pissed at me after the way I kicked him out last week. Or about the fact that I never called to apologize.

But I didn't want to talk to him. I didn't want to remind myself that he knew.

"Are you going to invite me in or should I just make myself comfortable out here?"

I grin. I can't help myself. "There's hardly enough room for two, but come on in."

He steps into the studio and I take a step back to give him space, but he follows me, backing me into a corner until he's leaning over me, his hands pressed into the wall, the heat of his body warming mine.

His eyes are on my mouth, but something hard and angry ticks in his jaw.

"Okay," I say, sighing dramatically. "I guess you can do me against the wall."

That earns me a smile. "Tempting, but that's not why I'm here."

No shit, I think, but I say, "That's disappointing." I cock my head. Pretending to be unaffected by his nearness is too damn hard. Asher is heat and passion and wicked indulgence. He makes me unsteady. "You wanted to help me work?"

He shoots a glance over his shoulder to my growing pile of broken glass and ceramic. "Is that what you were doing?" He steps away to examine my worktable. "What is this stuff?"

I catch my breath and find my footing. "Tesserae," I explain. "I'll use them to make mosaics."

"Wow." Glass tinkles as he sifts through the piles of raw material. "What kind of design are you going to make with all of this?"

I shrug. "I don't know. I only know there's something beautiful there. I'll find it."

He studies a piece of pink-streaked crystal against the midday light coming in the window. It clatters as he settles it back onto the tray and turns to me. "When I found you at the river—"

I cut him off with the shake of my head. "I want you to forget about that day. Please."

"You were wearing a ring. You were alone but you were wearing someone's ring." His gaze drops to my hand and his breath catches. "Jesus, Maggie. What happened?"

I lift my bandaged hand and shake my head. "It's no big deal. I just had an accident with the glass."

He takes my hand in his and examines the bandage. "Stitches?"

"A few."

He nods, satisfied, then surprises me by bringing it to his mouth and pressing his lips against the bandage. This man looks so rough and continues to surprise me with his sweetness.

"Who is he?"

I blink, lost in my contemplation of Asher. "Who?"

"Whose ring were you wearing, Maggie?"

"Oh, we're back on that." I shake my head. "I'm not involved with anyone if that's what you're worried about."

"It was that guy who married your sister."

"They aren't married. Engaged. The first wedding was botched, remember?"

"He was engaged to you first." It's not a question

I back into the wall, trying to get away from the conversation, from his frightening perceptiveness. "We were engaged last spring," I admit. "Whirlwind romance between old friends followed by a brief engagement. I called off the wedding when…"

"Because of the miscarriage," he says, piecing it together.

I don't correct him.

"But he's with your sister now." In only two steps he's against me again, but this time his leg is between my thighs, his hands at my waist.

"He's with Krystal," I manage, but I don't want to think about Will or Krystal.

I want to think about the way Asher's hands are curling into my ass, those eyes hot on me. I want to think about releasing him from his jeans and putting my mouth on him again. I want to think about him fucking me against this wall, hard and long, until I forget.

He presses closer, shifts my weight so it's almost entirely against his thigh. My eyes nearly roll back in my head from that simple, delicious pressure.

"And what about you?" he asks. "Are you over him?" One hand snakes up my shirt to graze the underside of my breast, the other knots in my hair. He tilts my head up until my eyes connect with his.

There's a quiet tap on the door, and I realize I've left it open at the same moment I see Will walk into the studio.

I push Asher's hands from my shirt. He steps back, eyes narrow, jaw ticking.

"Sorry to interrupt." Will runs his eyes over me, but he doesn't look sorry at all.

Asher's face has gone stony. Mine is hot, and my breathing is uneven.

"I wanted to check on you," Will says. "How's your hand?"

"Better. It's making working difficult, but there's plenty I can do with just my right hand." That's a lie. I can't do shit with my right hand, but I don't want him to worry.

Will nods and starts to leave, but he stops himself and turns back to us. "Maggie, take the internship." His eyes flick to Asher then back to me. "I never would have had the courage to take the leap to start the gallery if you hadn't given me permission to dream big."

Asher slides his fingers through mine. "Of course she will."

I blink at him.

Will nods, his jaw set in a tight line. "Great." Then he backs out of the too-small studio.

Once we're alone, I spin on Asher. "You don't get to speak for me."

"Do you want to work in the gallery?"

"Yes, but—"

"Take the internship. Don't let them take your dream. Be part of it."

My shoulders drop and I close my eyes. "It's not that simple."

"Because you still want him?"

My eyes fly open. "Why would you say that?"

"He still wants you," Asher growls.

"He's marrying my sister."

He lifts a dark brow. "That doesn't change the way he looks at you. Or the fact that he'd like to kill me."

I step forward and grab a fistful of his shirt, pulling him toward me.

He leans down obediently, until his mouth is a breath from mine.

"I like you, Asher. But if we're going to keep this up, whatever *this* is, you need to know my life is a little fucked up. *I'm* fucked up."

His eyes search mine. "Then we're a great match."

Asher

She pushes me away before I can kiss her. "You don't know what fucked up is." She turns to the window, and the sunlight splashes across her freckles, making her look as young as she is.

"Try me."

She whips around and, for a second, I think she might tell me—something, anything other than the shit she shovels to everyone. But then she pastes that smile on her face and shrugs. "Nothing you couldn't hear from the magpies down at the beauty shop."

"And the story they'd tell me, does it involve your ex-fiancé?"

"Of course." Her smile is so manufactured her face looks almost plastic. "A rush to the altar and a runaway bride? Does it get any better than that?"

"But would it be the truth?"

That clears away her smile.

My gaze drops to her bandaged hand and wrist. "Was that about him?"

"What?" She pulls her hand against her chest. "This was an accident."

"Yeah?" I take her hand. She doesn't protest, but she watches me with a tight jaw as I remove the splint to find the swollen, neatly stitched wound.

My heart pounds at the sight of the stitches that run from the base of her palm right onto her wrist. I want to scream, to rage, to punch the asshole who drove her to this. Instead, I re-secure the splint.

"Someday," I say softly, "you'll tell me the whole story. I'll wait."

"When you know the whole story, you won't want me anymore. I'm that kind of girl."

"Don't count on that."

When I lift my eyes to her face, she's watching me with something like wonder. "What?"

She shakes her head. "I can't figure you out."

"Good." I cup her face in my palms and trace her bottom lip with my thumb. "Then maybe you won't be able to figure out how to push me away."

Maggie

I can't create shit with my left hand immobilized, and the doctor wants me to keep the splint on any time I'm working until the wound has a chance to heal more. After Asher left, I was determined to lose myself in my work, making sense of little shards of glass and ceramic, but I'm so damn frustrated at my limited fine motor skills that I'm ready to throw something.

Whatever. I'm a mess anyway. There's some mysterious flower growing outside my art studio window that doesn't agree with my allergies, and at this point there's nothing but a drugstore for some allergy meds in store for my evening.

I lock up my studio and I sneeze for the tenth time in as many seconds.

Asher wants me to open up. I get that. He wants to know me. With any other girl, it would be the logical thing to want, but he doesn't understand what he's asking from me. Not even Will knows the whole truth. He doesn't understand that he doesn't *want* to know the real me.

As I turn toward the exit, I smack right into Ethan Bauer.

We jump back simultaneously.

"Maggie." His lips curve into a smile on my name.

Damn, damn, damn. I have no desire to talk to him.

"Ethan."

His eyes skim over me, and the hot gaze that used to make me wildly reckless with need now only makes me feel disgusted.

"There are nubile undergrads to seduce down this hall today," I say with my sweetest smile.

He winces. "I'm heading to the bathroom."

"Well, there it is," I say, pointing. Again. A smile.

"Nubile undergrads? You really think that little of me?"

Déjà vu.

"You really think that I don't love you? With all my heart I love you. I want to be with you. I want to wake up next to you in the morning."

All lies, of course.

I want to turn on my heel and leave, but I stand my ground.

"You never did have a very high opinion of me." Then he disappears into the bathroom.

He doesn't know how wrong he is. Once, I had a very high opinion of him. Too high.

The first time I posed nude for Dr. Ethan Bauer, I was so at ease, he'd asked me to return. So many models, he explained, were too modest to do some of the more earthy and sensual poses he'd been itching to capture on canvas. *I* would be perfect.

So I posed for him.

"I'm going to ask you to do some things, Maggie, to get you where I want you."

"Okay." I flashed him a daring smile. "I'm not modest, Bauer. I don't know what you're so worried about."

"You're lovely."

I peeled off my dress and he handed me a man's dress shirt. "Put this on?"

"Should I be worried that the artist who was supposed to paint me nude wants me to put clothes on?" I laughed as I slipped the worn cotton shirt over my shoulders.

It smelled like him. And that day, as I inhaled that musky scent, I admitted to myself that I had a crush on him, the notorious womanizer Ethan Bauer.

My fingers moved to the buttons and his gruff voice stopped me. "Don't," he whispered.

"Ah, I see," I said.

"Do you?" He led me to the small couch. "Because I want to see you, Maggie. And if that makes you uncomfortable, I want you to tell me. You need to be comfortable for this to work."

I laughed. "I've already laid myself out naked for you. I can't imagine what you think might make me uncomfortable about posing with a shirt half on."

He didn't reply but situated me so I sat sideways on the couch, legs bent slightly, the shirt covering my breasts.

"Look to the left," he said, clicking on a new light.

He returned to his canvas and studied me. "Beautiful. Are you okay?"

"Maybe you're the one that's too modest, Ethan," I laughed. "I'm fine. Paint, already."

"I'd like you to move your right hand, Maggie. As if you were about to touch yourself."

His words buzzed through me and sent heat to pool in my belly. My nipples tightened under the soft cotton of his shirt as I cupped myself between my legs. "Like this?"

His chest rose, fell, rose again. "You're perfect." He crossed to me, spoke in soothing tones. "We don't want to give it to them. We want to taunt."

He moved my hand, pulling it up so that my palm lay against the flat of my belly, my fingertips just above the thatch of hair between my legs.

"This isn't really my style," I said, eyes on his. "I don't exactly need to sneak up on it."

He chuckled, his face inches from mine, his smile sending that heat circling lower.

If he had moved in first, I may have been turned off. If he had closed the distance between our lips, the next year would have unfolded differently. Maybe I would have gone to more parties. Maybe I'd have followed Lizzy to Brady's a little more often and had a harmless affair with a young townie—maybe some guy I went to school with or a recently divorced physics teacher from New Hope High School. Maybe I'd have given William Bailey the chance he deserved instead of cornering him into a marriage neither of us was ready for. But Ethan didn't make a move toward me.

I recognized the heat in his eyes, and it made me hot, made me feel powerful. In that moment, I wasn't so foolish as to think he might someday leave his wife for one of his students. That would come later. After hours of lovemaking, hundreds of paintings he would never show. His secret obsession, he called me.

At that moment, it wasn't about anything but hot, thick, blood-pumping feminine power. I lifted my head just enough to brush my lips across his. I kissed him, this man I thought so highly of, I was willing to overlook the wedding band on his finger.

I take a deep breath and exhale deliberately, as if to blow away the memory.

Regret holds me in its claws for a few stuttering heartbeats.

Ethan emerges from the bathroom and I freeze. When our eyes lock, the warmth I once felt for him is gone. Those soft gray eyes seem to be pleading me to deny it, to validate his always-faltering self-worth.

"What do you want from me, Ethan?"

"Honestly?"

I let out a puff of air. "I asked, didn't I?"

"Let me take you to dinner. There's so much we never said." His gaze does that roaming, conquering thing again. I want to tell him to keep his eyes to himself, but that would mean admitting I notice.

My eyes began to water, another sneezing attack coming on. "I'd rather not," I say, but it sounds more like *Ud wathur wot*.

Ethan steps forward and reaches for my face. "Don't cry."

The pressure builds further in my head. I grab his wrist to push him away, and William Bailey turns the corner.

Will takes in my face, my tears, Ethan's hand. "What's going on here?"

Ethan drops his hand as if my face was suddenly burning him.

"Maggie, I don't want you seeing him," Will says, hard eyes on Ethan. "He's trouble."

Ethan nails me with the intense gaze that once got me in so much trouble. A moment later, Will's eyes lock with mine. If Ethan's gaze says, "I want you," Will's says, "I need you. I'm incomplete without you."

chapter ten

William

MAGGIE WALKS into the gallery dressed in cut-offs that show more thigh than they cover and a tiny tank top, and I nearly drop a piece of stained glass off my ladder at the sight.

"I'm ready to work," she announces, spreading her arms. "Use me and abuse me."

Having her here is a really bad idea.

I shoot a guilty glance over my shoulder toward the back office, but Krystal's not here. She went over to campus to talk to someone about another painting that she seems to think we need for the opening.

"I'll be done in a minute," I call down from the ladder.

"You mind if I take a look at what you have here?"

"Knock yourself out."

I carefully hang the piece of stained glass from the wire line, pretending I'm not completely shaken by her presence. Floor-to-ceiling windows overlook the river and flood the gallery with light. The stained glass will draw everyone's eye here. I center it carefully before climbing down to greet her.

When I reach the bottom of the ladder, I wipe my damp palms on my jeans.

With a slow spin, she smiles. God, she's practically glowing today. Did Asher Logan do that?

"This photography is amazing." She sits by a box in the middle of the gallery, folding her legs under her as she sorts through artwork.

"He's out of Chicago," I say, motioning to the photos. They've been mounted to stainless steel and make for perfect additions to sleek, contemporary interior designs. They are made to be displayed in panels of three. But which pieces to display at the opening? I haven't decided yet. Maggie was always better at finding themes in collections of art. I'm better off behind the camera.

"What are you thinking for prices?"

I hand her the pricing binder and she scans the columns. "These are really reasonable rates for this kind of talent, but I don't want to scare people away either. We always said we were going to have art for everyone, right?" She tilts her head to look at me and a red curl falls in her face. I make a fist to resist the urge to tuck it behind her ear. She blinks, as if realizing her error. "Of course, maybe you and Krystal weren't worried about that. I'm not trying to make my position more important than it is, I just—"

"Maggie." I hold up a hand. "Stop being so self conscious. We want you here because we value your ideas."

She grins and my shoulders relax. It's such a damn relief to have some of this tension gone between us. "Okay," she says, "because I was thinking we could do a sampling of his different sizes for the opening—that way someone on a budget might still be able to take some of his photography home. Not to mention we could make a nice balance of small and large pieces along that wall."

"Sounds good." Tucking my hands into my pockets, I step closer to examine the photographs she's chosen. "Listen, the house is done."

Her head snaps up and she looks at me with wide eyes.

"Our house. Krystal's and mine," I say hastily, then wish I could pull the words back. I hired the contractor to build the house when Maggie and I got engaged and just never stopped the process when she left.

I study a painting because I can't bear to watch her. "We've been living there for a while, but I think the finishing touches are finally all in place. We're doing a housewarming party this weekend. We wanted to invite you."

"I'll see you then," she says, and I can hear the forced smile in her voice. "What were you going to do with the little room off the front?" She hops off the floor and wanders over to the paintings leaning against the far wall. "I *adore* this watercolor series, and I think it would look great with the lighting in that room."

I swallow. Hard. "We promised to feature Professor Bauer in that room."

Her hands freeze on a watercolor of a little girl in white. "Oh." The tremor in her hand is barely perceptible, but I see it.

"It's just that he helped us get the grant to open the gallery," I explain.

She tucks her hands in her pockets—to hide that they're shaking? "Of course! And, gosh, with that talent why wouldn't you feature him?" She turns a small circle. "Where is his collection?"

You can't protect her, Will. "He's going through his paintings now. He's going to make his own selections."

She gives a tenuous smile. "I would expect no less from the illustrious Ethan Bauer."

I swallow and step away from her. She smells too damn good today. "He's being really damn secretive about his collection. He insists he can't set it up until the morning of the opening, and he wants to stage it himself."

That happy glow seems to slip right off her face. "Why would he do that?"

I lift a shoulder. "Krystal's chalking it up to his artistic temperament, but I don't like it any more than you do." I watch her carefully as I ask, "Do you have any idea what it might be?"

She shakes her head. "I'll talk to him, see what I can find out."

I know that costs her. She doesn't want to talk to Ethan Bauer any more than I do, but I also know he's more likely to talk to her than anyone else.

"It's just so hard to believe," she says as she scans the walls. "This is really happening. When we talked about it, I don't know if I ever really thought we'd do it. But you made it happen." She sets her eyes on me and pain slices across her features so damn clearly I feel like I've hit her. "You and Krystal, I mean."

The silence is awkward and unnatural between us, and I search for something to fill it. "I don't know if we're going to make it," I blurt before realizing I plan to share my problems with Maggie at all. "Me and Krystal? Our relationship is broken. I've done everything I can think but—Jesus, we're not even having sex and that was fine but it's like she doesn't even want me to touch her anymore."

Maggie dodges my eyes. "We shouldn't talk about this."

I release a bitter laugh. "I used to talk to you about all my girl problems."

"Will…"

"I'm thinking about calling off the wedding." Saying the words makes them more real, and as they slip from my lips anger and frustration and regret all rush through me in a flood so intense I can't tell them apart.

She blinks at me. "You are?"

"Yeah."

"What do you want?"

The only sound is the hum of the air conditioner as we stare at each other, and I feel that old addiction surge up, that need for a fix that silences every reasonable thought and makes me reckless until all I can hear is my blood in my ears and all I can think is of tasting her again.

Her tongue darts out to wet her lips before she pulls the bottom one between her teeth.

In two strides, I close the distance between us and pull her against me. Hard. It's stupid and impulsive, and I feel like I might die if I don't do it. But I do. Because last week's brush of lips did nothing to squelch this craving. It only left me wanting more.

I bury my hands in her hair, holding her tight as I slip my tongue between her lips in a kiss that's fueled by this mess of emotion pumping through me. Anger. Frustration. Regret. Her hand curls into my chest, and I pull her closer. I want her curves against me, need her under me. In this moment, my future and my plans mean nothing next to the pulsing need to *possess*. To take.

My hand slips under her shirt. When my mouth moves to her neck, I feel a shudder pass through her, and my dick aches from the unaccommodating confines of my jeans. God, I'd forgotten the rush of making this woman tremble.

"Don't," she whispers.

"It okay," I promise, snaking my hand up to her breast. Even to my own ears, I sound like a manipulative asshole, but only part of my brain registers what a scumbag I'm being. The rest of my mind is four steps ahead, getting her naked and getting inside her. Fucking her until I don't care anymore what a mess my life has become.

I can't register anything that doesn't get me to that goal. So my fingers are working their way to the clasp of her bra before I realize the hand on my chest isn't encouraging. It's pushing me away.

I loosen my hold on her a fraction and she takes the opportunity to shove me, harder this time, until I stumble back.

Her eyes blaze with anger as she lifts her hand to her lips. For a minute, I think it's heat I see there. Passion.

"*Never* do that again," she says. And it's the shaking in her voice that brings me to my senses. It's a shaking that has nothing to do with arousal.

"Oh, Jesus." My breathing is heavy and labored, and I stumble back a couple more steps as I struggle to get the air I need. "Jesus, Maggie. I'm sorry. I didn't think—"

"Didn't think I'd mind being your *whore*?" Her eyes glisten with tears. "Didn't think I'd mind you feeling me up while my *sister* wears your ring?"

"It's not like that and you know it." My jaw tightens. How dare she treat me like one of her asshole ex-lovers when I'm talking about giving up everything for her?

"It's not? Because that's what it feels like, Will. My sister won't fuck you so you came to me for a little something the first chance you got."

I throw up my hands. My dick aches and she's making me out to be trash when I haven't done a damn thing wrong. "Krystal and I are *broken*," I spit out between clenched teeth. "Broken because of how I feel about *you*."

"I don't care," she hisses. "I don't want you to touch me as long as your ring is on her finger."

"That little detail never seemed to bother you with any of your other men." The words are ugly and cruel. The second they're out of my mouth, I regret them, and when she flinches, I hate myself for them.

"Men?" she says softly.

I wince. Jesus, I'm an asshole. "What happened when you were in high school," I say slowly. "I know that wasn't your fault."

She crosses her arms and stares at me, eyes glistening as she waits for me to confess that I know more than she thought I did.

"But Maggie, you have to admit you have a pattern. The sheriff—"

"Fifteen, Will. I was *fifteen*."

I nod, slowly. I'm in dangerous territory here and I know it. "You weren't fifteen when you slept with Ethan Bauer," I say softly, and at her sharp inhale I realize she thought it was a secret. She really believed no one knew she was fucking her married art professor, her mentor, for most of her sophomore year at Sinclair. "And now Asher."

"What about Asher?"

"Well, for starters, he's a no-good piece of shit that only wants one thing from you."

"What?"

I don't repeat myself. I can tell by the anger in her eyes that she heard me just fine.

"You don't get to choose who I'm with, Will. You gave up that right when you shacked up with my sister."

Anger pumps through me at that. Thick and pulsing and hot. "Don't throw that in my face like I betrayed you. *You* called off our wedding, Maggie. *You* left town. What? Did you want me to run after you? Did you want me to *beg* for you to give us another chance? Because I tried, remember? I would have done whatever it took to keep you if I had thought it would work, but you shut me out. Stop making me out to be the villain. *You* left *me*."

"I had my *reasons*," she shouts.

"Yeah? Care to share those?" I wait for an answer I know she won't give me, my heart pounding. When I speak again, I lower my voice. "You don't have to be with me, but I'll be fucking damned before I let you lump me in with all the other assholes you've been with." I drag my hands through my hair. "Damn it, Maggie, why do you give so much to men like that?"

"Men like *what*?" Her arms are crossed tightly over her breasts, as if she has to protect herself from me. *Me.*

The notion is so absurd I almost laugh. I look her over—the thin tee, the short shorts, and for the hundredth time since she developed breasts, I wish I could mandate her wardrobe. I can't stand the things men in this town think about her, but worse is the way she does everything in her power to perpetuate the reputation.

"Men. Like. *What*?" she spits.

"Men who want you as their fuck toy and nothing else."

chapter eleven

Maggie

I AM in hell.

Krystal and Will's housewarming party is over the top. It features all
the luxuries that most women only dream of having for their weddings,
and only a very elite few enjoy for the sake of showing off their excessive
wealth to anyone they can con into attending.

Everyone is dressed to impress, the silver is polished, and the conversation is delightfully polite.

Asher is the evening's only saving grace and right now he's off playing nice with Aunt Kathy who was, apparently, a big fan.

Lizzy and Hanna are keeping me company and not attempting to
keep their greedy little eyes off my date. They both look stunning tonight, dressed in matching dark red dresses with halter necklines. They
may not look like twins, but from time to time, they like to dress the part
anyway.

Personally, I went for the strapless look. I like wearing dresses around
Asher. I like the way he can't keep his eyes off my legs. I can practically
hear his thoughts as he talks himself out of dragging me to a dark corner
to investigate what's underneath. I wish he didn't have such damn good
self-control.

I peel the fondant icing off a piece of cake. "God, whatever happened to good, old-fashioned butter cream frosting?"

Lizzy snorts. "They got rid of it when cake stopped being about taste and started being about appearance."

I hold a piece of yellow fondant against the flickering light of a candle. "It looks like plastic. I can't eat anything that color."

"Don't talk to me about food to me," Hanna grumbles. "I'm on a diet."

I roll my eyes. "Why?"

"Three words," she says. "Red. Leather. Pants."

"The ones you wore to Melinda's Halloween party two years ago?" I ask. "Are we talking about the ones so tight that I had to help you put them on *and* take it off?"

"I'm sorry. It sounds like I'm interrupting." Asher grins at the girls as he settles into the seat next to me.

"Kinda," I say, and at the same time Lizzy says, "Not at all."

Asher looks at me expectantly. "Don't let me interrupt. You were talking about peeling leather pants off each other?" He rests his chin on his hands. "Go on."

Lizzy beams. "Asher Logan," she says, offering her hand. "I'm Lizzy Thompson, and I hear you're a little freaky."

"Lizzy!" I swat her arm.

Asher quirks a brow. "I didn't figure your sister for the type to kiss and tell."

"I didn't tell her about the kitchen," I hiss.

"No, just about the night you met." Lizzy wriggles her eyebrows. "But tell me about the kitchen." She leans forward, leering just a little. "Please?"

Asher chuckles but my cheeks are an inferno of heat. Which is ridiculous because I'm not the type to be embarrassed about sex.

Hanna hums as she studies us, a crooked smile on her face. She tugs at Lizzy's arm. "We'll leave you two love birds alone for a bit."

When they're gone, I turn to Asher. He looks so damn sexy tonight. "You're coming home with me to attempt to redeem this night, aren't you?"

He grins at me. "I thought maybe we could make some coffee. You know, really talk and get to know each other." He winks and I melt a little inside.

"Asher Logan, if you think I'm going to walk around in these heels all night and not get anything out of it, you are mistaken."

He chuckles and kisses me on top of my head. "Maybe we can compromise."

"If your idea of compromise involves a lot of naked flesh, I'll consider it."

I don't get to hear his reply because Will has made his way to us. "Thank you for coming tonight. I told Maggie she didn't have to bring a date, but I suppose someone needs to keep her out of trouble."

Asher nods but murmurs so only I can hear, "I was more interested in getting you into it."

"Love the house," I manage. "Congratulations."

Will's eyes soften as he looks at me, and something tugs in my chest. Regret? Longing? Anger?

Next to me, Asher stiffens. He's too perceptive. As much as everyone else seems blind to it, he sees the way Will looks at me. Asher's seen it from that first night, and now tension rolls off him in tangible waves.

"I hope you're taking good care of Maggie," Will tells him.

"Maggie's not a child," Asher says stiffly. "She doesn't need to be taken care of."

"Everyone needs someone to take care of them," Will counters, eyes hard.

Asher folds his arms, refusing to take the bait.

After a couple of beats of awkward silence, Will says, "Let me know if I can get you anything."

Asher's jaw ticks, and we sit in silence for a minute after Will leaves us.

"I guess it's still a little awkward," I say.

"Because he still wants you."

101

William

Asher's hands are all over Maggie. In my house. He touches her at all times. A hand at the small of her back as they tour the house, his fingers laced through hers as they chat with guests by the bar, a finger along her jaw as he whispers something into her ear. And when they are pulled apart, it's worse. The looks she casts him across the room are charged with sexual tension. Want, need, and something tender.

I need a drink.

A soft smile curves Lizzy's lips. "I've never seen her so happy. They're adorable together."

I lean against the wall and watch the couple in question. *I want that.*

But even as I think it, I'm not sure which part I want. Do I want that easy chemistry between them? Do I wish that base attraction was part of my relationship with Krystal? Or do I want Maggie?

"Twenty says they sneak to the bathroom to do the dirty before the night's through," Lizzy says with a grin.

I force myself to return her smile. "That's a sucker bet."

"Maybe." She studies them, sipping at her glass of wine. "But Maggie's turning over a new leaf. I don't think fast and furious bathroom fucking is part of the New Maggie plan."

My silent questions are answered by the image that flashes fast and vivid through my mind. Maggie in the bathroom, her hips propped on the porcelain sink, her skirt bunched around her hips, head thrown back as she bites back a moan, her lover's fingers curling into her hips. But in my vision, they're not Asher's fingers. They're mine. And it's my name that slips from her lips as I press her up against the door and slide into her.

Fuck. What am I even doing?

Krystal comes into my line of vision and I feel like the piece of shit I am.

She's been avoiding me. We don't touch. We hardly talk.

If things hadn't already been finished between us, the receipt I found in her drawer tonight would have been enough to end things.

When I meet her eyes, I realize for the first time that she already knows it's over.

Maggie

I need some air, so I slip out the oversized French doors to the back of the house.

Just off the patio, lanterns line the cobblestone path to a lush garden. The thick air of Indiana summer weighs hot and heavy in my lungs.

I follow the path to a burbling fountain and find Will tucked in a corner, an unlit cigarette between his fingers.

"Aren't you going to go inside and mingle with your fiancée?" I ask softly, sinking into the wrought iron chair beside him.

"I needed a break from"—he waves a hand—"you know, everything."

I nod because I do know, and the silence stretches between us, comfortable for the first time since I came back.

He takes a breath. "Have you ever told anyone about the baby?"

Oh, Will. And it hurts so much—the words, the memory. The hurt never goes away, but this moment wrenches it to the surface like someone tore off the bandage and dug dirty nails into my wound.

I blink at him, but I can only think of the morning after my miscarriage scare. The ER doctor had done an ultrasound and shown me the baby's steadily beating heart. *Sometimes this happens. A blood clot. Baby's fine. No miscarriage.* Just a clot in my uterus and enough blood to keep me terrified for weeks.

The next morning, I woke up and stared at my wedding dress, as if it could make everything okay. As if it could make the lie I told Will true. As if it could make the decision I had in front of me any easier.

"No, I haven't." I meet his eyes—blue, soft, a little haunted. "Have you?"

"I think about him," he whispers.

Her, I think, and my heart breaks, shatters right there on the dregs of my own misery. He deserves to know the truth, but it would only hurt him more. "Me, too," and it's true. I think about *her* every day. "Asher... he also knows."

Will's brow wrinkles. "He does?"

"Yeah. He found me the day I went to the hospital."

"Oh." Hurt flashes in his eyes. "And you two have kept in touch?"

"No. I met him again at Krystal's wedding. We just put two and two together last week." Or Asher did. I didn't remember him. That morning at the river, he'd been inconsequential. I'd been too focused on my own fear.

"Oh. Right." He stares at the fountain. Thinking? Avoiding my gaze? I'm not sure. But then he says, "You know that I wasn't just marrying you for the baby, right?"

I swallow back that thickness in my throat. We'd been together for barely three weeks when I told him I was pregnant. I never would have accepted his ring so young if I hadn't been pregnant.

"I always wonder about that. If you understood how much I cared for you. If you just thought that you were saving me by ending it, leaving town."

"It was for the best."

He finally meets my eyes again. "I'm still in love with you."

I jump out of the chair. I don't want to hear this. "Don't."

I put several yards between us, pretending to examine the fountain. My fingers graze the water-slicked stone of the angel's face.

"Maggie. Is there something more I could have done? To keep you?" His voice is close, and I'm not surprised when I feel his hands on my shoulders, turning me. "It's over between me and Krystal. It will be over. Tonight."

My heart trips. Stumbles. Aches.

"You were right. I had no right to kiss you before I ended it, and I have no right to do it now."

I open my mouth to respond, to tell him he can do better than me and my lies.

But then his lips are on mine and he's kissing me.

It's not the hungry, demanding kiss from the gallery. It's nice. Soft. Gentle. If Will is anything, it's gentle. Maybe I need someone tough, someone hardened like me.

His lips brush mine once, twice, then he retreats. His fingertips trace down the side of my jaw. And I should be angry, but I'm not—not when his kiss makes me feel so safe.

When I pull back, Asher's standing five yards behind Will, his gaze locked on me.

"I thought I'd find you out here." His expression is guarded. "I'll be inside when you decide this is a bad idea."

My heart sinks and my stomach lurches. They collide inside me, my lungs a casualty, torn apart by the wreckage.

Why couldn't he look hurt? Crushed by my indiscretion? Anything but that guarded, you-can't-hurt-me look I understand so well.

He walks away and I ball my fists to resist running after him, resist the instinct to explain what can't be explained.

"He's no good for you, Maggie," Will says softly.

"That's not fair."

Will puts his finger to my lips and studies me. "I'm sorry." Does he mean for the kiss? For what he said about Asher? But he says, "I'm sorry I couldn't be what you needed. So sorry. You'll never know." And then he walks away.

And I'm alone with nothing but the taste of my regret and the weight of my lies for company.

Asher

I want to put a hole in the wall of William Bailey's fancy-ass house. I want to break his porcelain serving platters and shatter his crystal.

I want to *drink*.

It's the last that has me so damn unsteady, licking parched lips and watching the door as I wait for her to return. I'm not leaving without her. I'm not running from here with my tail tucked between my legs like he wants me to. He saw me coming and he kissed her to prove he could.

And she let him.

His lips were on Maggie, and I wanted to throw him across the yard, wanted the satisfaction of feeling my knuckles connect with his skull.

God. Damn. It.

Will approaches, his hands tucked into his pressed black dress pants.

I hate him so much in this moment I have to ball my hands into fists to keep from decking him.

He runs a hand through his blond hair as he looks distractedly around the party.

Jesus. This guy is class and style and reeks of old money.

I follow his gaze. Maggie has returned. She's twisted that flaming red hair off her neck, revealing the tender spot I know makes her crazy.

Will stares at her, naked longing in his eyes.

Maggie spots me and freezes, deer-in-the-headlights terror on her face. "I need a minute," she says, backing up a step. She looks to Will. "May I use your restroom?"

Will casts a glance over his shoulder. "I think Aunt Shirley's in that one. You can use the one off the master down the hall."

Will and I watch her leave. The tension between us angry enough to bruise.

"Stay away from Maggie," Will warns softly, his gaze on Maggie's retreating form. "She deserves better. Does she even know about Juliana?"

I don't give him the satisfaction of looking at him. My skin across my knuckles burns from my fists being balled so tightly. I force my hands to relax and walk away, going after Maggie without a word to this man who thinks he has some sort of hold over her.

I find her in the master bath. She's standing at the counter, hands pressed against its edge, head hanging. She doesn't look up. "Go away."

I flip the lock on the door before putting my hands to her waist. Our eyes meet in the mirror.

Her eyes blaze. "I'm *fucked up*, Asher. Don't you see that? I'm a fucking home-wrecking *slut*."

I watch her in the mirror as I trace the edge of her jaw with my thumb, leaning in to brush my lips against the smooth, exposed column of her neck.

Electricity.

It's there every time I touch her, and it whips through my veins in a violent, hungry rush. She feels it too. I can see it in her eyes. I can feel it in the way her body instinctively presses closer to mine.

She reaches back and threads her fingers through my hair. "Why are you even still here?"

Our eyes meet in the mirror again. I dip my fingers into the top of her strapless dress and feather them across her breasts. I want to peel it off her, spin her around and graze my teeth over her nipples, set her on the vanity, and open her legs to my mouth. "I care about you, Maggie."

She flinches, as if the words offend her. "You don't know me."

"Maybe not. But I understand you." I let my mouth hover over her ear. "Are you calling yourself a slut because you kissed him or because you know you're going to let me touch you in here?" I pause a beat to let that settle in. Blood pulses hot and thick into my dick at the catch in her breath. "I think you want me to. You want me to make you come in the house of the man you were going to marry."

I am insane with wanting her. I don't care where we are. I don't care that she's just kissed another man. I need this woman despite that.

Fuck all reason, I need her because of it.

I slide my hand up her dress, tracing the edge of her panties with my fingers.

Her hips buck and her back arches as she rocks toward me.

"Tell me you don't want me to take you here," I whisper. "Tell me you don't want me to bend you over this vanity. Tell me you don't want to watch in the mirror as I take you in his bathroom." I slide my fingers down the seam of her ass and cup her from behind.

She gasps and licks her lips. She's struggling to maintain control. "Yes," she breathes. "Please."

I press my lips to her ear. "Tell me that you care about me."

In the mirror, I watch her eyes flutter open. "What if I don't care about anyone?"

I move my hand, rub her, and I'm rewarded with a throaty moan. I could touch this woman for hours if she'd let me. I want to make her lose hold of that control she holds so close. I want to break down her walls.

I slide my fingers into her panties from behind. "You're so damn wet," I murmur, touching her clit.

She moans softly.

A knock sounds at the bathroom door.

"Maggie, are you okay in there?"

Maggie pushes my hand from between her legs and spins around. She grabs my shirt, holding me still.

"My mother," she whispers.

"Yes, Maggie, we're worried about you," another voice calls.

"And Granny," Maggie whispers.

I groan softly. *Nothing* could kill my hard-on right now, but the word *Granny* certainly kills the mood.

"Yeah, I'm okay. I just needed a minute alone."

"Maggie, are you sure that this isn't all just a reaction to seeing Will marry someone else?"

Good question, Granny.

Maggie shakes her head.

"Or maybe you're feeling bad about yourself because you see Krystal starting this great life and yours is in shambles."

"What about that nice man she's here with tonight?"

"Oh, let's not get ahead of ourselves," the other voice protests. "I can hardly see that working out."

"Maggie, even if it doesn't work out, I'm glad you're getting yourself some tail."

"Granny!" Maggie screeches, breaking her silence.

I chuckle silently and Maggie thumps me in the chest.

"I'm sorry, but a girl that young shouldn't keep herself cloistered."

Maggie rubs her hand over her eyes in obvious distress.

"So, what? You want her to tramp all over town?"

"Gretchen, sex is natural. God gave your daughter those parts for a reason."

"Yes, so she could get married to a good Catholic man and make good Catholic babies."

"But until she finds that man—"

"Mom! Granny! Please!" Maggie begs.

She shoots me a death glare when I have to bite back laughter.

Maggie turns on the sink and calls over the running water, "Give me a minute to wash my face, and I'll be out."

"Okay, dear."

"If there isn't anything we can get you."

The women's voices fade as one asks the other, "Where did her delicious-looking date run off to?"

As the sound of their steps fades, I let myself laugh. "They're quite a pair."

Maggie splashes water on her face. "They mean well. We should get back."

With a sigh, I nod toward the door. "Go ahead. I'll meet up with you in a few."

"Rumors are already probably flying that I ran in here in despair and I'm desperate to get Will back to fix my broken life."

A fist tightens in my chest at her words. "Are you?"

She closes her eyes. "No one can fix me, Asher. That includes you."

I let her leave. I let her shut me out. For now.

A few minutes later, I return to the party, but when I survey the room, I don't see Maggie anywhere.

"She left."

I turn to see Maggie's sister Krystal. "Left?"

She shakes her head. "Leave it to Maggie to leave a party without telling her date."

"It's kind of a kick in the balls," I admit.

Her face relaxes a little. "I'm a big fan, by the way, and that's kind of an awkward thing to admit to my little sister's boyfriend."

"Thanks." I arch a brow. "Did she call me her boyfriend?"

Krystal snorts. "Are you kidding? She's hardly talking to me. I stole her man, remember?"

"Hmm. That's not exactly how she explained it to me."

Silence stretches between us for a few beats before Krystal says, "I am sorry, you know. Everything's just so screwed up." She swallows and tears well up in her eyes. When she speaks again, I can hardly hear her. "Will's always been in love with Maggie, and I've always been in love with Will."

"And what about Maggie?"

Krystal frowns. "Maggie? Maggie's too busy hating herself to love anyone."

chapter twelve

William

"YOU SHOULD have told me that you didn't want to marry me," I tell Krystal.

She freezes in the middle of sliding a diamond stud from her ear. "What?"

Her lips part. For a minute I think she might feign ignorance, but instead, she sinks into the chair at her vanity and looks at her hands. "I do want to marry you."

Everyone's left for the night, and I can't put this conversation off anymore.

I study her in the mirror and feel hollow. She looks beautiful tonight. Her hair is pulled off her neck in some sort of twist, and she's wearing a long black dress that makes her look jaw-droppingly elegant. Under the dress, the bra and panties I bought her for Valentine's Day.

On paper, we are so good for each other. We're well-educated, like-minded, and we want the same things out of life. We love each other.

Why isn't that enough?

"If you want to marry me," I say slowly, "why did you sabotage our wedding?"

A teary streak of mascara runs down her face. Her lashes are damp with tears when she looks up at me. "Because you still love her." The words are matter of fact, not thrown like an insult or accusation, simply delivered like an unfortunate truth.

"But I love you too." My voice breaks on the words.

"I know you do."

"Then *why?*" I sink to my knees and take her hands in mine.

She threads her fingers through my hair. "I didn't want to live my life wondering if the man sleeping next to me would rather be sleeping next to someone else."

I squeeze my eyes shut, guilty of the crime. "I needed you to believe in me. In us. The wedding…it made me question everything. It made me question us."

"I needed time."

"Time for what?"

"To prove to myself that things were over between you and Maggie." She gives a sad smile. "But that's not what happened, and I realized I wasn't even living my own life. I was living the life you and Maggie had planned."

"Why didn't you just ask to postpone the wedding?"

"I was afraid you would think I was running away. Like she did."

Her hands are so soft. I kiss each knuckle, then I open her hand and press her palm to my lips.

"It's over, isn't it?" she asks.

"I never thought it would end like this."

She squeezes my hand. "We can't pretend that this is enough anymore."

The silence cracks with a ragged sob. Hers? Mine? I wrap my arms around her waist and lay my head in her lap. She combs her fingers through my hair as she cries.

I know she's right, but that doesn't make this hurt any less. "I'm sorry. I'm so sorry I couldn't let her go."

Minutes pass with nothing but our breath and her tears filling the silence, then Krystal gently pushes me back and pastes on a smile. "We're both going to be fine."

I stare at her, the reality of what has just happened settling in further with each beat of my heart. "Will you stay on? Continue to be a part of the gallery?"

She gives a sad smile. "I'll be there through the opening. After…" She shakes her head. "It was never my dream. It was yours and Maggie's. I was just the understudy."

Maggie

She won't stop crying and no one can calm her down.

"He was so perfect. Why do things have to fall apart like this? Why can't people just live happily ever after?" She draws in a long, shaky breath and wipes her snotty nose.

Lizzy casts a pleading look at me over her shoulder before returning to patting and cooing. "Everything happens for a reason. Krystal's going to be okay, Mom."

I drag my hand over my face. Sunday morning brunch has been hijacked by the announcement of Krystal and Will's breakup. They delivered the news together, holding hands, and I thought how much stronger she is than I am.

When I called off my wedding, I didn't want to look at anyone, and I left town as quickly as I could. Not Krystal. She delivered the news with her shoulders back and her chin high. Then she and Will hugged before he left.

It would have been relatively painless if my mom wasn't so beside herself.

I turn away from mom's tears and run into Krystal. I've been avoiding her all morning, afraid she'd blame me.

"Can we talk outside?" she asks softly.

I nod and follow her out back. The sky is gray and it's drizzled on and off all morning. A year ago, when I told Will I couldn't go through with the wedding, the weather was like this. We walked by the river, letting the rain disguise our tears as I fed him small pieces of the truth.

I told him about how much I bled at the river and that I went to the hospital. I didn't tell him it wasn't a miscarriage.

I told him it was okay because I wasn't ready to be a mom anyway. I didn't tell him I would be giving my baby to someone else.

I told him I felt like I'd pushed him into marrying me. I didn't tell him that the baby wasn't his.

The memory makes me cold and I freeze in my tracks at the deck steps.

Krystal's halfway down the path to the river before she realizes I've stopped. She turns and waves me down. "Come on, Mags."

I swallow and push myself forward to catch up. When I reach her, she doesn't say anything but continues walking. Neither of us speaks until we're stepping onto the dock.

"I was always so jealous of you," she says softly.

"What?" My oldest sister is about as perfect as a person can get. I can't imagine why she would have ever been jealous of me. "Why?"

She shrugs. "You were the fun one, the cool one. Even when you were young and Will didn't see you as anything more than a kid, he loved to be around you."

"He hung around all of us," I object. "Not just me."

"I was the boring one."

"You're not boring."

Her eyes connect to mine. She looks so tired. "It's okay. It wasn't your fault you shined so bright."

I swallow hard. "You think I shined bright?"

"Brighter than the sun since the day you were born," she whispers. "It's not your fault that Will's still in love with you."

"Oh, Krys."

"I don't blame you anymore." She takes a breath. "I used to, but I don't anymore."

My heart squeezes in my chest and I don't know what to say.

"I blame myself. I knew he was in love with you, but I wanted him anyway. I told myself it was okay because you left." She shakes her head. "But it wasn't okay. He's always been yours."

The forgiveness is in her eyes, and it hurts too much. I walk to the end of the dock and look out into the water. A raindrop hits my cheek and another hits my shoulder, but I don't turn back to the house.

"Will you try to go back to Will?" she asks. "Once everything settles down?"

I watch the rain hit the water, watch the tiny drop get swallowed up by the water. My tongue is heavy, as if it's weighed down by wet sand from the river's bottom.

"You don't have to tell me, obviously," she says, "but I know he'd take you in a heartbeat."

Krystal is offering me a gift that I can't take. Being with Will would mean I would have to tell him the truth—and the secrets I've kept from him, I don't think he could ever forgive.

chapter thirteen

Asher

A KNOCK at my door pulls me from sleep. I roll over and look at the clock.

Five a.m. is way too damn early for company.

I drag myself from under the covers, grabbing a pair of jeans off the floor and tugging them on as I make my way to the door. I'm in my apartment in New York, a place I keep for the sole purpose of the one week a month I get to keep my daughter. If it weren't for her, I'd get rid of the damn place. New York is toxic to me, but I won't spend the little time I get with Zoe in a damn hotel room.

The knock sounds again.

"I'm coming," I mutter, pulling the door open without checking the peephole.

Juliana stands on the other side, her mouth drawn into a pout, annoyance coloring her features.

I cross my arms. "Do you have any idea what time it is?"

"Sure, I'd love to come in. You're such a gentleman." She pushes past me and into the apartment, and my mind is filled with flashes of memories from the days we lived here together. We'd party and roll in about this time and barely make it through the door before we fucked.

Now I never bring women here, and instead of weed and beer bottles, the living room is littered with pink toys.

Suddenly, she turns her appraising eyes to me, my bare chest. Her smile is approving. And a little lopsided. "What do you know?"

"Not much before a decent cup of coffee," I mutter, ignoring the heat in her eyes and the suggestion of her smile. If I'm guessing right, Juliana is drunk or close to it.

Her eyes drop to my crotch. "You're looking good, Asher. So good I haven't stopped thinking about you since you came by the house this afternoon."

I sigh and point to the clock. "That would be yesterday."

"Such a stickler for details."

"Where's Zoe?"

"At home in bed."

My jaw ticks.

"What? The nanny's there. She's *fine*."

"Juliana, you need to understand something."

Her eyes are on my lips as she closes the space between us and trails her fingers over my bare chest. "Yeah? Is it something good?"

Bile rises in my throat as I remove her hand. "I don't come to town to see you."

She rolls her eyes. "Come on, I know you get a little randy in the mornings." This time, both her hands are on me and she looks up at me through her lashes. "Let's have a little fun." She shimmies her body closer and presses her breasts against my chest. "I miss the way you fuck me."

I clench my jaw and fist my hands at my sides. My brain wants nothing to do with this woman, but Mr. Balls For Brains down south has other ideas.

"Come on," she whispers. "Remember how good it used to be."

"Stop," I snarl, stepping back. "I don't remember, and neither do you. We were too goddamn wasted to remember shit. You're with Chad now, remember?" *Chad.* I can barely speak the man's name without spitting. I've come a long way in the last year, and I take responsibility for my actions. But I still hate that man's guts.

She drops her hands and scowls. "Jesus, you've become such a buzzkill."

I don't respond. I don't care enough to argue any more. "My lawyer sent you papers."

She's weaving her way toward the door. "I'm going to pretend he didn't," she says. "You'll change your mind."

"No, I won't." But she's already out the door.

The sun blazes hot in the morning sky, and I slip my sunglasses on as I ring the doorbell of the brick monstrosity. The yard is well tended, the gardens lush. Hell, the inside better be in great shape too, since I pay for it all.

Juliana opens the door with a smile that drops from her face the moment she sets her bright brown eyes on me. She's hardly the same woman who stumbled into my apartment this morning. "What are you doing here?"

"I'm here to see Zoe."

Her face turns icy, and she throws a worried glance over her shoulder. Looking for her little guard dog of a boyfriend, no doubt. But I checked to make sure Chad's car wasn't here before I came up to the door. That little protective order he has against me makes it tricky to see my kid.

"You know you aren't permitted—"

"Juliana—"

"No, Asher. Don't. You're the one who screwed up here."

"I don't—"

"Daddy?"

Zoe's standing at the bottom of the staircase, tugging on a pigtail.

The jagged edge of something broken snags my breath from my lungs. I drop to a knee and open my arms.

She gives me a tentative smile before scurrying toward me with a shriek of delight. She throws herself into my arms and clings to me and that jagged edge rips through me and tears away the rest of my numbness.

"Just look at your beautiful new house," I whisper. "I bet you haven't even seen the whole thing, it's so big!"

She giggles. "Have too!"

"I think it's a castle."

"Nuh-uh!" She puts her hands on her hips.

"Sure it is! A big house where a princess lives is a castle."

"It's not a castle, silly!"

"Zoe, why don't you go play in your room?" Juliana says.

"Do you wanna see it, Daddy?" Zoe asks, those milk-chocolate eyes widening.

I kiss her forehead. "Not today, sweetie."

"When do we get another special day?" my daughter asks, backing toward the stairs.

"Tomorrow after piano lessons. I'll pick you up."

She grins and hurries up the steps, taking half of my heart with her.

"Why do you do this?" Juliana demands.

I watch Zoe until she's out of sight then turn to Juliana. "Do what, exactly?"

She frowns and softens the edge in her voice. "Show up here when you know it's against the court order? Get your daughter excited about seeing you before it's your visitation time?"

"Because she's my daughter," I growl. I take a step back. My fists clench at my sides and I feel the old anger rising up in me. "I have a right to see her."

"You do. One week a month."

I take another step back and shake my head. "She's my daughter."

"What if Chad had been here?" She lifts her palms. "Asher…"

But I don't want to hear what she has to say, and I head to my car before I say something I'll regret.

chapter fourteen

Maggie

"I'M GONNA need another," I sing as our waitress comes by our table.

Hanna and Lizzy exchange a look.

"What about you two?" the waitress asks.

"We're fine," Lizzy says, eyeing my nearly empty glass.

"What?" I ask, leaning forward on the table. "Are we having a good time tonight or not?"

"Just take it easy, okay?" Hanna says.

The Friday night crowd is an odd mix of townies and college kids who stayed in town for a job or summer classes. I'm not even sure which category my sisters and I fit into. Are we townies because we grew up here or did we start to get lumped in with the pretentious assholes when we started at Sinclair?

"I'm not spending my Friday night holding your hair while you barf into Brady's toilet."

I roll my eyes. "Lightweights."

I talked my sisters into moving martini night to Brady's, where we're dancing instead of gossiping and drinking cheap margaritas instead of martinis. I almost canceled in favor of some vodka and solitude in my studio, but I thought better of it when I remembered how that ended last time.

I want to talk to them about Krystal and Will's breakup. I want to show them the pictures of Grace that came in the mail this week. I want to ask if they know why Asher wasn't pissed at me when he saw Will kissing me last week.

I want to talk to them like a normal girl talks to her sisters. Maybe, if I have one more drink, I can.

"Maggie," Lizzy calls, waving a hand in front of my face. "Don't leave us, girlie."

Hanna's frowning. "What's on your mind, Mags?"

I blink at her and smile. "I need to know how to seduce a rock star."

I've begun thirty-two text messages to him this week. Thirty-two times, I picked up my phone and pulled up his number. Thirty-two times I deleted the message before sending it.

I want to end whatever this is between us. Other than Will, Asher is the only one in New Hope who knows about my pregnancy. And then he saw me kiss Will and he didn't get pissed. I'm terrified of how much he knows about me, how much he *sees* when he looks at me.

But no matter how many times I tell myself that his disappearance from my life is for the best, every thought circles back to him.

Hanna and Lizzy are staring at me with wide eyes.

"What? Can you blame me?"

They exchange a look. "We just thought..." Hanna begins.

"...Based on the way you two *look* at each other," Lizzy says before Hanna chimes in with, "We assumed you already..."

"You know," Lizzy finishes.

"He won't," I whine.

"Well, there's been plenty of eye-fucking between you," Lizzy says. "We can attest to that."

I groan. "Lotta good that does me. But, hell, I probably screwed up my chance when I abandoned him at Krystal and Will's housewarming. He hasn't called or anything."

Lizzy chokes on a sip of margarita, her eyes watering. "You left him there?"

"Why would you *leave* Asher Logan?" Hanna asks.

Lizzy scowls at me. "We are living vicariously through you right now.

I cannot stress how important this is. Don't screw it up for us by acting like that."

"I panicked," I admit.

"About *what*, exactly?" Lizzy asks. "Because that man *wanted* you."

I think of Asher's penetrating gaze, his attempts to knock me off balance, the way he sees more than anyone else. I wave away the question. I don't know if I could explain *sober*, let alone now while words elude my grasp.

"Wait," Hanna says. "You said *he* hasn't called *you*? Have you tried to contact him?"

I cross my arms. "I thought he might be pissed."

"Yeah, and that's why you start with an apology." Lizzy snorts and extends her hand, palm up. "Give me your phone."

"No," I say, but Hanna is tossing something to Lizzy across the table. "Hey, give it back!"

"If you can't be trusted to do this right, then we'll do it for you." Her fingers are already flying across my screen, and as hard as I try, I can't scowl enough to stop her. "There," she says, handing my phone back.

I snatch it from her hand and open my texts to see what she's done.

I'm at Brady's. Wanna fuck?

Hanna peeks over my shoulder and bursts into laughter as my jaw drops.

"I thought you said I need to *apologize*?"

"Bet you it works," Lizzy says with a smirk.

"I could kill you," I mutter.

She grins. "You could text him again and let him know your sister stole your phone or you could wait and see what he says. Either way, you're contacting him *and* dealing with the sex question. It's a win-win."

The murderous rage I'm feeling must be showing on my face because she hops out of the booth. "I love this song! Han-Han, let's dance!"

They scurry off to the space in front of the jukebox that we treat as our dance floor, and I'm left smiling despite myself.

The margaritas are catching up with me, and I can't ignore it much longer, so I head to the restroom. Krystal made sure her little sisters knew early on about the assholes who took advantage of girls' neglected drinks at parties and bars, so I'm sure to take mine with me.

I weave my way through bar patrons and back toward the dark hallway that holds the bathrooms.

"Hey, Lucy," a deep voice calls.

I ignore it at first, but the hand on my ass has me grabbing a wrist and spinning around.

A chill spreads over my skin and sweet and sour mix rolls in my stomach. I release his wrist and step back. "What do you want, Kenneth?"

"Nothing," he says, raking his eyes over me and making me feel exposed in my tank and jean skirt. "Not right now at least."

I curl my lip—"Not ever."—and turn toward the bathroom.

I take care of business, wash my hands, and then turn the water cold before splashing my face to cool it, to wash away the memories of being the fifteen-year-old girl the high school boys nicknamed "Lucy." When I close my eyes, I can still hear them calling out from their lockers, can still feel their knowing eyes on me as I walked down the hall. I can still remember my dad learning about it and telling me, *You get the reputation you earn.*

When the shaking in my hands settles, I pour my drink down the drain. With assholes like Kenny around, the last thing I need is to be blurry-eyed by booze. Or *more* blurry-eyed, as the case may be.

Guys like Kenny made my high school years hell, and I'll be damned if I'm going to let them have that much control over me as an adult.

I exit the bathroom cautiously, worried Kenny might be waiting. But the hallway is empty and I have to laugh at myself when I see him leaning over the pool table. He's not a threat. And if he tries to touch me again, I'll just remind him what I do to the balls of men who grab my ass without permission.

It's a speech I save for special occasions, but it involves scissors, origami, and a staple gun, and it works like a charm.

The twins are dancing, and I almost want to sneak out, too afraid my mood will erase those beautiful smiles from their faces. I make my way to the dance floor anyway, and force a smile as I sway to the beat.

My eyes are closed when I feel someone press against me from behind. After my interaction with Kenny, I'm jumpy and I stiffen immediately.

"It's just me, gorgeous."

My shoulders relax at the familiar sound of Asher's deep voice, and I melt into him and the music, letting his arms wrap around my waist.

I turn in to face him and wrap my arms around his neck and his hands drop to my sides and tighten on my hips.

"Now isn't *that* something," Kenny calls from the pool table. He's looking us over and shaking his head. "Fucking rock star millionaire and he's sleeping with the easiest lay in town. You like 'em loose, Asher?"

Asher freezes and his body goes so stiff against me, I might as well be dancing with a piece of granite.

"Ignore him," I whisper. "He's nobody."

Asher brushes my hair back and presses a kiss to my forehead. "Be right back."

I wrap my fingers around his biceps and squeeze. "Please. Don't. For me."

His jaw is hard as he glares at Kenny across the bar.

"I gotta bounce," Kenny announces, pulling on his coat.

I tighten my hold on Asher's arm. He could escape me if he wanted. I know that. But I don't want him talking to Kenny. I don't want him giving Kenny the satisfaction of the fight he's itching for.

Asher's body is tense and he watches Kenny until he's out the door. Only then does he turn back to me and pull me into his arms.

I peer up at him through my lashes. "I'm sorry about that."

"It's not your fault." The words are ground out through clenched teeth, and his muscles are still tense under my fingers.

"My reputation comes from the choices I made. I'm responsible."

"No one deserves to be treated like that."

There's nothing I can say, so we dance together in silence until the tick in his jaw lets up and his rigid muscles soften.

When the song changes to something slower, he says, "I was a little surprised to get your text. I hope you haven't been looking for me. I've been out of town all week, just flew back in tonight."

"I thought you might be angry with me," I say softly.

"For abandoning me with your family, people I hardly know? What guy doesn't love that?"

I laugh. "Okay. It was pretty shitty of me."

"You're forgiven," he says, brushing my hair from my face.

"So, do you always come when summoned?" I grin. "Or are you finally going to sleep with me?"

His eyes drop to my mouth. "You only summon me when you're drunk."

"It was actually my sisters this time." I lean my head on his shoulder. "Are you going to use that as an excuse again? Because I'm actually not drunk at all. Just…well lubricated."

"You know that's not the only thing stopping me."

"You know too much about me," I whisper. "I don't blame you for not wanting me. You've seen too much of who I really am." Oh God, that sounds like such a pathetic plea for attention that I don't even have to wait till morning to hate myself for it.

He groans, tugging me against him until I can feel the hard ridge of his erection against my belly. "Maggie." His mouth is at my ear, a rush of heat as he breathes my name. "Do you think I don't want the same thing you do?"

His voice is low, for my ears only, and it sends a wicked whip of pleasure through me.

"Do you think I don't close my eyes and remember exactly what it feels like to slide my hand between your legs? To feel you, wet and swollen for me?"

My breath catches on his words and my heart pounds. I have to avert my eyes. Looking at him while he says these things is too much, too intense.

"Do you think I haven't thought about what it's going to be like to spread your legs and taste you?"

My breath hisses out of me, and I look up to see his hot eyes watching me.

"I want to be inside you, Maggie. I want you in my arms and in my bed, and I'll have you there." He twirls a lock of hair in his fingers and tugs gently until I lift my chin and look into his eyes again.

I swallow. "What's stopping you?"

His eyes drift across the bar and I'm not surprised to see them land on Will. This is Will's favorite place. Is that why I keep coming here? Because I know he'll show up?

"You saw him kiss me," I say. "Why don't you hate me?"

The sway of Asher's hips stalls for two heartbeats before he resumes our dance as if I've said nothing.

"I kissed him. Didn't you see that? I was there with you and I kissed him."

"Why do you need me to be angry with you?" He trails his fingers down my sides, brushes his thumbs over my belly, his fingertips over the curve of my hip.

"You know things." I step back away from his touch to make sure he's hearing me. "You know things that no one else knows. That no one else *can* know. Do you understand that? You shouldn't want to be with me. You should want to be with someone…better."

"Fuck *should*. I want you." His hands are on me again and I feel like I'm walking along the edge of a steep precipice, like I might slip over the edge and lose control.

"I keep waiting for you to stop showing up," I say. "To give up on me."

"Do you want me to give up? Because I saw the way he was looking at you last week, Maggie. If you want him, he's yours."

I blink. Krystal had said the same thing, but they don't understand that it's not that simple. "And what if I want you?" I ask softly.

"I'm here, aren't I?"

"You are. You keep coming back. For what? What is this between us?"

He slides a hand into my hair and leads me to lean into him again. "It's whatever you want it to be, gorgeous. With one exception."

"What's that?"

"It's not just sex. *That's* why I won't sleep with you. I won't *let* this be just sex."

That makes me smile. "Why me, Asher? I'm just some small-town slut with too much baggage. You could have anyone." I can feel his heart beating against my cheek and its steady pace increases at my question. "Why me?"

"Sweetheart, when you know the answer to that question, we won't be talking anymore."

I pull back and blink at him. "You'll be gone?"

His lips quirk. "I'll be inside you."

Asher

Maggie feels so amazing in my arms. I don't want to let her go, even if we are dancing in the middle of a rundown bar. I bury my nose in her hair and inhale deeply. She has me so addicted to her scent, I'm surprised I haven't tracked down her shampoo for a daily hit.

"We're getting another round," Lizzy calls from the bar. "You need one, Mags?"

Maggie cuts her eyes to me before shaking her head.

"You don't have to stop drinking for me," I say softly.

"I know. But it's okay. I'm done."

"What about you, Asher?" Lizzy asks.

"I've got everything I need right here," I call back, tightening my arms around Maggie.

"Want to sit?" Maggie asks.

I nod and follow her to a booth. She grins when I slide into the same side with her, thighs touching.

When I wrap an arm around her, she settles into me, and I see her ex watching us from across the bar. For the first time, though, Maggie doesn't seem to notice or care.

"Why don't you drink?" she asks, peering up through her lashes. "If you don't mind me asking."

"It's a condition of my probation."

She inhales sharply.

"What, like it's a secret?"

"I…" She licks her lips. "I didn't think you'd want to talk about it."

"My past is ugly, and I'm not proud of it, but it's part of who I am. It made me who I am. I'm not hiding from it."

She ducks out from under my arm and wraps her arms around herself. "No one's asking you to."

I squeeze my eyes shut. "I'm doing a fine job of fucking up an otherwise perfect night, aren't I?" I open my eyes again when I feel her fingers on mine.

"I won't judge you for your mistakes, Asher. I'm the last person who would do that."

I intertwine my fingers with hers and squeeze her hand. My heart knots painfully in my chest with something I can't name. "I did it," I say. "I'm not some innocent dude being punished for a crime he didn't commit. I did it."

"Were you drunk?"

"Yes. Drunk. High." The silence grows heavy between us as I let the ugliness rise up. I examine it with such detachment now. "You've read the reports, I'm sure. I was drunk and out for blood."

"I haven't read them." She shrugs. "I don't care to. You aren't that guy, Asher."

Her confidence shakes me, and I have to swallow back this feeling in my throat I know she wouldn't like.

"So, probation? What does that mean?"

"For me it meant anger management classes, and weekly drug and alcohol screening." And a protective order that keeps me from seeing my daughter any time I want.

She blinks. "Wow. That sucks."

I lift a shoulder. "It beats the alternative."

"Which was what?"

"A year in prison for aggravated battery."

"A year?" she says softly. "But you definitely don't have to serve time, right?"

I shrug. "Assuming I can stay on the right side of the law for another month, sure." I force a smile. "But that's why I'm in New Hope and not at my house in the city. Easy enough to stay out of trouble here."

She snorts. "Depends who you talk to."

I squeeze her hand.

"What happens if you get in trouble with the law while you're on probation?"

I take a breath. "I have to serve my year sentence." And worse, I'd miss a whole year with my daughter.

She's silent the entire drive home. I pull into the driveway of her rental and shut off the ignition.

I want to stay with her tonight. I want to kiss away the memory of

Will and any other man who hurt her. I want to take her slowly and softly in her bed. I want to hold her, because—whether she'll admit it or not—that's what she needs.

She's looking out her window, not at me, and the soft tension of unspoken secrets hisses like steam in the silence.

"I have a daughter," I say into the darkness. "She's four years old, and smart and amazing, and because her mother is living with the man I assaulted, I can only see her during my one week of visitation a month."

"A daughter?"

"That's why I wasn't around this week," I explain. "I flew to New York for my week with her."

"I had no idea."

I swallow, not entirely sure why I'm sharing all of this. "I want primary custody, but my lawyer said going after that while I'm on probation is asking to lose. So I'm waiting, but she's my world."

She's still not looking at me, but if my having a child scares her away, so be it. Zoe has to come first.

"You're not the only one who's made mistakes. I have too. But I believe we're more than the sum of our mistakes. I didn't used to. I thought I was a piece of shit. I thought I was nothing." I take her hand and lightly brush my thumb over the gauze wrapping her wrist. "I used to drink to feel numb, but then I sobered up and a different kind of numbness followed. It was Zoe who made me feel again, and who made me believe I was more than the sum of my mistakes."

"You're lucky." Her voice shakes. I wonder if she's cried since that day at the river. I wonder if this might be the moment she breaks. What does it say about me that I want her to? I want her to break so I can find her in the pieces, just like she does with her mosaics.

She laughs but it sounds crazed, maniacal, but then she looks out the window and whispers, "Oh, my gosh," and there's a smile in her voice.

The streetlight slants in the window, giving me just enough light to make out her changing expression.

"What is it?"

"That's Krystal's car." She slumps down in her seat, and the light catches on her earring, making it flash in the darkness.

I follow her gaze to the red Mini Cooper parked down the block. "Is she visiting you?"

"Not me," Maggie breathes. "That's Tyler's house."

"Who's Tyler?"

Maggie chews on her lip, masking her smile. "Tyler was her first love."

Krystal steps onto the softly lit porch, dressed in a tank and shorts that show off her long legs. She's quickly joined by a tall man in a dark t-shirt and jeans.

We watch as Tyler cups her jaw in his hands and kisses her softly.

She follows him in the door, and my chest is heavy with the implication of it.

"What will you do?" I ask.

Pulling her eyes from the illuminated scene, she turns to me. "What do you mean?"

"Will you tell him?"

She straightens. "Will and Krystal broke up the night of the housewarming. There's nothing to tell."

Will isn't engaged to her sister anymore, and she's here with me? "They broke up? For good?"

"Yes."

"And you're not with him?"

"No."

I lean across the seat and pull her against me, kissing her hard and hungry, because if she wanted her ex-fiancé back, she could have him. I slip my tongue between her lips and she opens to me, sliding her hands into my hair and kissing me back. Her lips are soft and her tongue hot, and I want so much more.

When we finally separate we're both breathing hard and the porch down the road is dark.

We get out of the car and hold hands as I walk her to the door.

"You want to come in?" she asks, and the need in her eyes is more than a physical reaction.

I brush my lips across hers. "Go let Lucy out. You're coming with me tonight."

chapter fifteen

Maggie

"Do you take all your girls here?" I ask Asher. But the humor fizzles out of my voice when I see him spread a blanket on the grass.

He brought me to his house and led me through the backyard and down to the river.

With most men, this wouldn't make me uncomfortable because knowing what they wanted, knowing where it was going, would give me a sense of control. Not with Asher. "I don't know what you want from me."

"I want you"—he tilts my chin toward the sky—"to look at these stars."

So I do. I turn and lean into his chest and look at the New Hope stars. The bright ones. The ones that are so faint they look more like a hint of light than a dedication to it. I find the big dipper. The little dipper. I listen to the soft rushing of the water and feel my shoulders relax and my breathing slow.

The silence stirs between us for a long time, intense with what hasn't been said, heavy with what I know I can't say. I wish to be someone else, a woman with an untainted past, a woman who could whisper secrets about her life with no real shame.

Finally, Asher speaks. "I'm not asking anything from you, Maggie. I'm a patient man. I know you've been hurt and don't feel like you have much to give."

And there it is again. That ache. That burn to explain. And maybe I would. If this were a different world or I were a different person. If I weren't so very afraid of what it might mean to trust him with the most fragile pieces of myself.

"Normally, I back off when I start to feel something for a woman. But the thing is"—he whispers now—"it's too late. I've already fallen for you."

My eyes fill with hot tears, and I duck his embrace and put space between us. I tell myself I'm not running away. I'm giving myself some much deserved space from a man who wants more from me than I can give.

I step closer to the river and slip off my shoes. Calm rushes through me at the slight give of the earth beneath my feet. The air is heavy with the smell of river. The scent of fresh water mixes with mildew and slowly decomposing earth. I love the smell, love the promise of it. That everything, no matter what its beginnings, has a purpose and will break down and become a part of something new. A tree limb will become part of the riverbed; a frog will become part of the rich soil that will nourish a baby tree until it grows into a great oak.

I sense Asher before I hear him. His fingers slip into mine before I acknowledge him. His big, solid hand warms my smaller one. I have to fight the temptation to pour all of my troubles out to him, to share my worries with this man.

I pull my hand away.

"I don't want to scare you away," he says. "But I'm not the kind of guy who keeps quiet when he feels something. Not anymore." His voice is soft, soothing. A balm to my frayed nerves.

"I'm just not there, Asher. I don't fall in love that easily." *And you don't want the likes of me loving you.*

"Not since Will?"

I don't know how to answer that.

"So many secrets." He sighs heavily. "Love isn't a bartering tool. I just wanted to tell you. I don't expect anything in return. Nothing at all."

I lean against him in the darkness and wrap my arms around his waist. "I didn't say I can't give you anything," I say, pressing my mouth against his chest, kissing my way down.

He draws in a breath. "The girl may be stingy with her love, but she's free with her sexual favors."

I freeze at his words, and he stiffens, seeming to register what he said. "I'm sorry, Maggie, that was uncalled for."

A sharp stab of pain—of shame—darts through me.

I look out over the water. "Maybe. But it's true. But maybe I'm cheap. Easy."

"Maggie—"

"Don't. Don't say it's not true. Don't rewrite history to make me feel better about myself."

His hand settles on my shoulder. "You give your body freely. That may be true. And you may do your damnedest to keep that heart hidden from the rest of the world. But it's not cold. You've got a great big heart, Maggie. So big that it peeks out from that place where you try to hide it."

A hot tear streaks down my cheek. "How can you believe that?"

He pulls me into his arms, presses my cheek into his chest. "Because I've seen it."

I run my thumb along the faint stubble covering his jaw, and he stares at me, like he's waiting for me to say something, like he needs me to say something. I lift onto my tiptoes and press my lips to his.

The contact is brief but electric. Does he know how badly I want to let him love me? How badly I wish I could love him in return? Once I believed myself incapable of loving. I thought it my sacrifice, the payment for my sins. But I feel it inside me—transformation. Something that was once so hard bending into something pliable. Something that, like the sandy earth beneath my feet, is flexible, can give a little.

Nervous with possibility, I shiver.

"Do you want to go inside?" he asks, running his hands over my bare arms. "Are you cold?"

I'm perfect. The Indiana heat dances in the night air. I let my cheek find his chest again. "Can we stay for a while?"

"Absolutely." Then he dips to take my mouth, and this time we linger.

His touch is soft, gentle. He runs his tongue along my lips, and I open under him. He tastes me, moves into my mouth, slants over me. His hands settle on my back, pressing our bodies closer. I feel utterly cherished.

When he breaks the kiss, a small cry slips from my lips. The river rushes by, the crickets sing, occasionally the hoot of an owl joins the melody, and Asher kisses my neck like he was born to do it.

I lace my fingers through his hair and lead him back up until his mouth meets mine again.

Dear God, this man tastes good. Like the warmth he puts in my belly and the spice he inspires lower. And he kisses like a god. His thumbs caress the small of my back until my head spins and my knees weaken.

He pulls away and takes my hand. Wordlessly, he leads me to the blanket and pulls his shirt off over his head.

"What are you—"

Before I can finish, he turns to me and removes my shirt, unbuttons my skirt and slips it from my hips.

I reach for the button on his pants, but he stops my hands, lifting them to the sides as he admires my body in the faint light of the quarter moon. The smartass comment dies on my lips, and I let myself enjoy his admiration. Unclasping my bra, I let it fall away.

His breath rushes out of him, but instead of the cheap thrill of sexual power, more of that insane liquid warmth fills my belly.

His thumb brushes across a hardened nipple before he peels away my panties.

He drops to his knees in front of me and finds me with his fingers, rubbing my clit and making me rock unsteadily on my feet.

He replaces his hand with his mouth. The wet flick of his tongue, light at first, then firmer, more insistent. A moan escapes my lips, mingles with the owl calls, and dissipates in the thick, humid air. When I think my knees can no longer hold me up, Asher scoops me into his arms and pulls my naked body against his bare chest.

At another time, in another place, I might have mocked him for this old-fashioned gesture, but right now—as he slowly lowers me onto the blanket, and I can feel the dampness of the earth seep through it—it's perfect. It's exactly what I need.

He discards his shoes and pants, never taking his eyes from me. Never ceasing his exploration of my body with his gaze, he rolls on a condom.

When he lowers onto me, I welcome his weight. I spread my legs so he can settle between them. Eyes locked with mine, he slides into me, and the air leaves my lungs as he fills me. Pleasure stretches its long fingers through me—strokes, caresses, awakens my hardened heart in the hot palm of its hand.

We find our rhythm like that. Asher, never taking his eyes from mine as he moves with me under the light of the waxing moon. Me, flooded with emotion spilling from my newly wakened heart.

Because I'm not a virgin. But this is all new to me. Here. With Asher in the moonlight, rough and hungry and dangerous. Exposed. This is making love.

Asher's fingers thread through my hair, and he pulls my body against his. We've moved into his bed, and we're tangled in his silky satin sheets, tangled in each other.

"I've never been any good at this part," I whisper.

Asher releases a contented sigh. He doesn't share my aversion to post-coital snuggling. "What part?"

"Cuddling. Pillow talk."

"There's nothing to be good at, Maggie," Asher whispers, nestling his nose in the crook of my neck. "Nothing to do. Just be."

I've never felt as exposed during sex as I felt tonight, and yet I'm finding myself less afraid to share in the aftermath. Less afraid the man I just gave myself to might really see me. Usually, I find myself lying there in awkward silence mentally battling the words of my father's ghost.

Whore. Slut. Loose woman.

That's slow coming tonight, but I'm waiting for it.

I inhale. Exhale. Repeat. My muscles relax incrementally. Asher's arm wraps around my waist and I feel his breath against my ear, feel his chest rise and fall against my back. I melt a little.

"I have you," he murmurs. "You're safe with me."

"Of course, I—"

"You don't need to pretend to be strong with me, Maggie. Just *be.*"

I close my eyes and brace myself to fail at this simple task.

Asher's knuckles brush over my belly.

My father's voice isn't here, condemning me. Nothing echoes in my ears. No images of blood-stained hands flit behind my eyes. No memories of my baby being taken from my arms in a suspended moment that feels like I'm being robbed of my soul.

I'm right here with the steady rhythm of Asher's breath and the soft brush of his fingers against my skin.

"You're good to me, and that scares me. I don't deserve you."

"You deserve better," he growls.

I'm surprised to realize how much I like this. How good it feels to have the warmth of his body against mine, his breath against my neck.

His arm tightens around me. "Why do you call yourself a slut?"

"Because I am," I say softly.

He doesn't reply, and his silence is a challenge I can't refuse. Not with this man.

So I explain. "You can only swallow ugly words about yourself so many times before they become part of your DNA. Some girls are told they're important, so it becomes part of them. Some are told they're talented or ugly or fat or special. It's a self-fulfilling prophecy. Me? I'm a slut."

"Tell me who made you believe that."

The room is quiet, save for the whir of the air conditioner and the soft slide of skin against satin sheets. I feel safe here, and for a minute I wonder how my life would have been different if tonight with Asher *had* been my first time.

"I started sleeping with my father's best friend when I was fifteen."

As if I flipped a switch, Asher stiffens against me. "What?"

I find his hand with mine and thread my fingers through his. "Dad was strict with all of us. About the way we dressed, about the music we listened to. The only difference was that I disregarded his rules. I liked tight jeans and low-cut tops. I liked *boys*."

Dad's voice is in my head again, so I focus on the heat of Asher's skin, the feel of his fingers in my hair. "I know now what I didn't understand then. That first time…" I draw in a ragged breath, exhale slowly. Asher's fingers comb my hair. "I didn't understand what was happening. Not really. I mean, I liked this guy, trusted him. Everyone did. He was the county sheriff and a family friend. He was my father's best friend. And I liked him so much that I would find excuses to go to his house. It wasn't all that uncommon for me to hang out over there, and his wife was gone a lot. She's a lawyer, and she was ambitious and worked all the time. Then one day we were watching a movie and he poured me a glass of sweet wine. I drank and we watched. I remember we were laughing about something, and suddenly he was doing things and whispering things, and I knew it was wrong but I also knew he was…in charge? And when it was over, I cried. I cried so hard I made myself throw up."

"Maggie." Asher's fingers curl into my waist but he doesn't pull away. Outside of a psychologist's office, I've never told anyone this story. I've never wanted to. Who would want to be involved with someone as broken as me?

"He was so mad at me. Why was I crying? I was acting like a child and he was sorry he'd made the mistake of treating me like a *woman* when I was going to act like no more than a girl. I was the one who kept coming around in tight jeans and low-cut tops. I was the one who flirted with him. I'd *wanted* it."

"Fucking. Bastard." Asher sits up in bed and pulls me against his chest. I lean into him, soothed by the searing heat of his anger.

"I knew he was manipulating me. Partly. But he was also partly right."

"No."

I shake my head against his chest. "He wasn't lying, you know? I liked him. I liked the way he looked at me. It made me feel…special. I knew what outfits he liked—he told me—and I'd wear them when I'd be around him. I *did* flirt with him. But I was just a kid and when he told me that wanting that attention meant I was asking for sex—meant that I *owed* him sex—I believed him." I have to stop. I have to breathe and remember that it's over. Remember that Toby is gone.

Asher doesn't push me. He holds me and waits.

"I knew he'd forced me to have sex. I knew I told him no. But I didn't understand it as rape. Not then. Not when this was a man I'd never been afraid of. It wasn't rape, it was me being a stupid girl."

"Did you tell your parents?"

"I was terrified of them finding out. Terrified what they'd think of me." I shake my head. "Considering I'd driven him to do it, I didn't know how to tell them. "

"You didn't drive him to do anything. He was a grown man in control of his own actions."

Hearing those words feels so good.

For years, I have told myself I knew what was right and wrong. I didn't need anyone's platitudes. But that was a lie. I need this. I need to tell Asher. "The next time—when he said he needed me, when he said it was our secret, when he said I made him lose his mind and he couldn't help himself—I cried the whole time. I just lay there with my hands fisted in the blankets and I thought—if I can just let him do this to me, if I can just pretend it's okay and make sure no one finds out, everything will be all right." I take in a shaky breath. "I've always been lonely. I don't fit in with my family, and I was afraid of losing this man who had become a friend."

Asher is holding me so tightly it almost hurts, but it's the good kind of hurt. It's a pain that reminds me I'm alive and I'm *worth* something.

"It went on for a few months before my dad caught us. I would find excuses not to go over there. Toby would find excuses for us to be together. When my dad caught us, for a minute I thought everything would be okay. I was *relieved*. My daddy was strict as hell but he loved me, and I thought he was going to make everything okay."

"But he didn't."

This is the part that hurts the most, and I close my eyes against the pain and concentrate on the rise and fall of Asher's chest. "Dad wanted to believe it was my fault. He needed to believe it. He needed to believe his little girl hadn't been raped, needed to believe his best friend wouldn't do that. So he told himself Toby's story was true. I'd taunted him. I'd begged for it. I'd seduced him. Everyone in town loved Toby. He could have had his pick of grown women, so who would believe that he'd force himself on a fifteen-year-old?"

I stop the flow of words tumbling from my lips to take a breath, to focus on the here, the now, the feel of Asher's arms before I continue. "Somehow the story got out. His wife left him and he left town, and everyone thought it was my fault."

"You were fifteen." When Asher says it, it sounds so simple. There's no way he can understand how much I need his faith in me. Even six years later.

Again I find myself wishing I could send him back in time to my teenage self. She needed him even more.

"My dad died later that year." I hate this part—discussing how my mistakes destroyed my father and my family. "He had a heart attack and died. The stress of it all…it was just too much for him. Will was the only one willing to speak up and stand up for me, but he was at college. For months after we buried my dad, my mom couldn't look me in the eye."

He brushes my hair from my face and presses a kiss to my forehead. "It wasn't your fault, Maggie."

"I know that," I whisper.

He slides a lock of my hair between his fingers. "Do you?"

"I'm not a kid anymore," I object. "Of course I know…" I trail off because he's not some therapist I have to convince, and he deserves more from me than the same bullshit I've been shoveling all my life. "I told you I'm fucked up, Asher."

"You're beautiful," he whispers.

"That's superficial. It's meaningless."

"Sometimes. But your beauty? It's the kind that radiates from your heart, Maggie, and it's so damn bright it shines beyond these walls you've erected to protect yourself."

I think of Will's words. *"If you're broken, I'll fix you."* Will didn't even know the whole truth when he made that promise, but he believed I needed fixing. "If I'm not a slut, I don't even know who I am."

Asher rolls me onto my back until his body is over mine, my face framed in his hands. "Don't be afraid to break, Maggie. Stop holding on to the ugliness just to stay whole."

Hot tears slip from the corners of my eyes and roll into my ears. "What if no one can fix me?"

"You don't need fixing." He gives a sad smile and wipes a tear away with his thumb. "It's like your mosaics. The beauty is already there, you just find it. Let go, sweetheart."

"I'm afraid I'll shatter."

He lifts my hand to his lips and kisses along the line of the stitches running down my palm. "If you shatter, I'll find you."

My eyes fill at his words, but he doesn't try to stop it. He doesn't ask me not to cry, he gives me permission to. He lies beside me, pulls me against his bare chest, until I'm baptized by silent tears.

chapter sixteen

Maggie

I WAKE up to an empty bed and the soft sounds of an acoustic guitar.

Asher's bedroom is gorgeous in the morning light. One wall is almost entirely windows looking out onto the backyard and the river beyond, not to mention the beauty within the room. It's sparsely furnished with a walnut king-size bed, end tables, and armoire, and the ceilings are vaulted, adding to the spacious and airy quality, as if it's an extension of the outdoor space.

I pull one of his t-shirts over my head and pad down the hall, toward the sound of the soft notes and low murmurs of song.

I find him with his guitar on the other side of the house, watching his fingers as he thrums the strings and sings softly under his breath. I can't make out the words, but I know they're beautiful because Asher made them.

I don't let him know I'm here at first. He's gorgeous like this. In jeans, his feet and chest bare, the guitar cradled in his arms so natural it looks more like a piece of him than an instrument.

As if sensing me, he lifts his head and smiles. "Hey, gorgeous. I hope I didn't wake you." He sets the guitar down beside him and stands.

"Don't stop for me." I bite my lip. "I was enjoying watching you."

He shrugs, looking a little self-conscious for the first time since I met him. "It's new, and I'm not ready to share yet. How'd you sleep?"

I grin. "So well. I don't think I've slept that well since I was five."

"Good." He pulls me against him, trapping my arms between our bodies. "Then maybe I can talk you into sleeping here again."

I hum, considering. "Maybe…"

"Can I feed you? I'm not the best cook, but my housekeeper keeps the freezer stocked with some pretty delicious choices and I know how to work the microwave."

"Tempting, but I have to be at the gallery in a little under an hour. We need to finish staging and inventory before the grand opening."

He brushes his mouth against my neck, no doubt leaving beard burn behind.

"How's that going, anyway?" he asks.

I moan, much less interested in talking about the gallery than I am in letting his lips continue their exploration. "It's going fine."

The heat of his mouth leaves my neck, and I open my eyes to find him staring at me.

"What?"

"He kissed you the other night."

I swallow, shifting back half a step. "I've mentioned that."

"Do you want him to do it again?"

I take another step back. I don't want to have this conversation. "Things are over between me and Will."

"You're not answering my question."

I open my mouth to shoot back a smart retort but I can't find one. "Are you seriously jealous?"

Before I can blink, he has me pressed against the wall and his mouth is on mine, rough and possessive. Hands driving into my hair, he shifts me until his leg is between my thighs.

I open under him, wanting his kiss and touch as much as I want to escape our conversation. More. He wraps my hair in his fist and tugs lightly until I open further, press deeper into the kiss.

When I am breathing hard and my legs are shaking, he releases me. I have to lean against the wall for support while I catch my breath.

"What was that?" I ask, chest heaving, my body protesting that there *must* be more where that came from.

"Just a little something to remember me." He winks and walks out of the room. Then, when he's halfway down the hall, he calls, "Tell Will I said hi."

William

She's humming under her breath and smiling while she takes notes in the inventory binder. She's wearing little black pants that stop just below her knees and a flowy tank top. She'd look almost innocent in that outfit if her ponytail didn't show the beard burn on her neck.

I haven't seen her this happy since last spring when I kissed her for the first time, and just the memory of that kiss is enough to make me hard.

"I think it's really coming together," she says, smiling up at me.

I blink at her, too busy thinking about how she got those marks at her neck. For a minute, I don't know what she's talking about. "Oh, the gallery?"

"The gallery." She frowns, studying me. "Are you okay?" She drops the binder on the desk. "How are you holding up?"

I stare at her for a beat. I don't know if she really expects me to answer or if the question is a courtesy. "I'm okay. It sucks, but it'll pass."

I wait for her to ask if I ended it for her, but she doesn't.

I guess we both know I did. At this point, the only question is if Maggie wanted me to.

"I pulled some strings in the department," I say cautiously. "I found a way to get your scholarship back."

Her jaw drops. "Really?"

"You know how I was trying to get you to switch to art education? If you change your major now, you could apply for this art education scholarship that's only available for established students."

The smile falls from her face. "I don't want to do art education."

"I know, you're MFA all the way, but think about the future, Mags."

"I am thinking about the future. I have no desire to spend the rest of my life in a high school."

"You'd be great. Stop letting that old story define you. Everyone else has moved on. It's your turn now."

She takes a step back, her green eyes hard. "Fuck. You. Those were the worst years of my life."

I set my jaw. "So, what? You're going to tinker with glass for a living? Find many job listings for that?"

"Fuck off," she growls. "I know you did the sensible business degree before your MFA, but I'm not you, and I didn't ask for your input."

"I'm trying to help."

"You're trying to fix me," she spits. "You know what? Some people don't think I'm broken."

"Who? Asher? Right, because he's one to judge how fucked up someone's life is."

"Don't act like you know him. You don't."

I laugh. "Oh, and you do? Come on, Maggie. How well can you really know him? What do you know about him? You know his family? Or his plans for the next ten years? Did he tell you what happened with the guy he beat to a pulp?"

"He doesn't have to tell me that."

My lip curls in disgust. "I bet he's found time to fuck you though."

When I register the hot sting of her hand connecting with my cheek, I'm glad. Because I deserve it.

Maggie

My hand shakes as I raise it to knock on Ethan Bauer's studio door. I haven't stopped shaking since I left Will and his nasty implications about my relationship with Asher, and to add insult to injury, now I have to talk to Ethan.

I want to pretend that coming here is no big deal, but I have too many memories in this studio. Too many mistakes. I don't want to be reminded how stupid I was to believe the things he told me, how naïve I'd been to hope.

Yet that hope is peeking into my consciousness again lately. When Asher lies beside me. When he touches me.

Is Will right? Am I being naïve?

I stomp down the thought and knock. Without waiting for him to invite me, I open it.

Oh, no.

A young girl's in front of the window, a red satin sheet wrapped around her, her dark hair swept up off her neck, her bare shoulders exposed.

"Maggie?" Ethan calmly puts his brush down.

The girl turns, eyes wide, as if she's been caught doing something much more scandalous than posing for the artist.

I understand. Posing for Ethan Bauer is much more erotic than the touch of most men.

"Ethan," I say. God, I want to be out of here, and soon. "We need to talk." No need to waste time on pleasantries.

"Um, I—" the girl cuts herself off with a quick shake of her head and reaches for her clothes. "I'll give you two some privacy."

I have things to say to Ethan that I don't intend on sharing with anyone else. On the other hand, I don't want to be alone with him. "Stay. I won't be long."

Ethan wipes his hands on the damp towel that hangs from his easel and the smell of paint thinner stings my nose. Red smudges disappear from his hands and stain the towel. Images blip through my mind. My hands covered in paint—the reds and yellows of tulips—and running over his bare chest. Then another blip of my hands covered in red. But blood, not paint.

I push back the unwelcome images and walk to the window where the model had been posing. It has a great view of the wooded ridge that runs along this part of the riverbank—the very best view of any studio at Sinclair.

Only the best for the great Ethan Bauer.

Aspiring artists from all over the country come to Sinclair for the opportunity to paint with Ethan. Some of them probably even make it through without sleeping with him.

The girl sits on the couch, looking uncomfortable as hell in her red sheet.

"What can I do for you Maggie?" Ethan asks. Those blue eyes, usually so hot, so intense, are cold.

"I need to know what you did with the Discovery collection." That's what he had called the paintings of me. And I'd been so flattered.

His eyes narrow. "It's not about you, Maggie. You can't decide you're going to keep art from the world because you're feeling self-conscious. It's not about you. It's art."

God save me from artistic egos. "Are you showing the collection at Will and Krystal's gallery?"

"It doesn't concern you."

Worry, dread, and horror fight for control over my more sensitive organs. "Where are they?"

The girl stands and scrambles for her clothes. "Maybe I should go."

I shoot her a look over my shoulder. "You need to hear this. Someday you'll be the one wishing you could hide the evidence of your affair with him."

Her cheeks blaze.

A month ago, I would never have said that. But after Will threw it in my face, the pretense seems almost ridiculous.

"Let me take you to dinner," Ethan says. "We'll talk. I want to know what projects you've been working on."

"I'll pass." I back out of the office, glaring at him as I go.

If he won't tell me where the Discovery collection is, I'll find out for myself.

Asher

Maggie pops another grape in her mouth before taking another sip of champagne. She's sitting on the solid walnut monstrosity that is my dining room table, her soft thighs showing beneath the hem of an old Infinite Gray t-shirt. For years, I've thought this space—with its ostentatious chandelier and heavy furniture—a waste, but sitting at the table with Maggie propped before me, I don't think there's a single spot in this house I like more.

"Your house is amazing," she says.

I raise a brow. "What? You didn't let yourself in when you helped yourself to my pool?"

She smacks me across the chest and grins. "Totally different. The pool is outside."

"But the sauna is in the basement," I say, gently parting her legs and positioning myself between them.

"Sauna?" She wriggles forward and wraps her legs around my waist. "How did I miss that?"

I am making myself hold back. I was almost surprised when she showed up at my door tonight, and I gave her the grand tour since we never got around to that last night. As we went from room to room, she was throwing come-hither looks over her shoulder, but I've held back because she's more than that to me, and I won't be like the men who have made her think that's all she has to offer.

So I break a slice of Havarti and pretend I'm not about to lose my mind when she uses tongue and teeth to take it from my fingers. "I think you were too distracted by the Cezanne outside the wine cellar to notice the sauna."

"Oh, I was distracted all right." She locks her feet together behind my back and pulls me closer. "But the painting was only part of the equation."

I offer her a grape this time, and her mouth is hot on my fingers as she takes it with her tongue.

"You like feeding me, don't you?"

"Among other things."

"You have a good eye for art," she says, and I know it's a compliment, considering the source. "Would you be interested in driving up to Chicago with me tomorrow? I need to check out a gallery up there."

I brush my lips over hers. "I'd love that."

She takes another sip of her champagne then frowns at her glass. "You don't drink, but it's not just because of the probation."

"Is that a question?"

She sets her glass on the counter and wraps her arms around my neck. "An observation."

"Do you want to ask a question?"

"Are you an alcoholic?"

I used to deny the label, but I've made my peace with it. The difference a year makes. "Yes."

She runs her thumb along my two-day growth of beard. "Then why do you keep alcohol in your house?"

"Because I won't let it have that kind of power over me."

"But it did before."

"Yes."

"What happened with the guy you assaulted? What did he do?"

I tense. "I told you, I was loaded."

She narrows her eyes. "There was a reason. He did something."

I can feel the hardness in my own jaw from thinking about Chad. "He was sleeping with Juliana. I found out and didn't handle it well."

"Juliana?" she asks softly.

I open my mouth and hesitate before answering. "Zoe's mom."

Her fingers wrap around my forearm and squeeze. "Does it bother you when I drink?"

"No," I say, but she must see something in my eyes because she pulls back.

She drops her legs from my waist and settles her hands on the edge of the table. "It does bother you."

"It bothers me when you get drunk, not when you have *a drink*."

She swallows and shifts her eyes to the abstract painting that covers the side wall. "Do you want me to stop?"

I stand and take her jaw in my hand, turning her to face me. Her big green eyes are rimmed with tears. "I'm not trying to change you, Maggie. I'm trying to love you."

She grabs a handful of my shirt and tugs me close. "Kiss me."

I want to kiss her. Taste her. Cherish her. When she told me about her past last night, it explained so much, and my chest still aches with hurt for her.

"This is more than sex, isn't it, Asher?" she asks softly.

"How can you ask that?" I run my thumb along the edge of her jaw. "I told you last night. I'm in love with you."

Her chest rises with her shaky inhale.

"Do you believe me?"

"I do."

I lower my mouth to hers, and I'm so damn hungry for this, my hands are on her before I even decide to let this be more than a kiss. I curl my fingers into her ass and draw her against me. I run my lips and tongue and teeth along her neck, and her fingers curl into my hair.

She's so sweet and I could taste her for hours. I want to take her to my bed and keep her there. I test her reaction to my fingers, my mouth, my tongue and my teeth. Lifting her arms, I pull off the t-shirt she donned when we toured through my bedroom. I slip it over her head and toss it across the table.

Her nipples are hard and taut in the cool air.

"You are so fucking perfect," I murmur, trailing my fingertips between her breasts and over her belly.

"Hardly," she whispers, voice weak.

As I lower myself, my mouth follows the path of my fingers, and I circle her navel with my tongue. Tiny silvery scars snake out from here. As I taste each one, she tenses under me.

"Stretch marks," she says softly, dropping her hands to disguise them. "Not so perfect."

I move her hands. "Perfect." And I kiss her there again, mouth, tongue, teeth. When I scrape my teeth across the ridge of her hipbone, she cries out and her moan echoes off the walls.

"I fucking love that I can do that to you." My breathing is choppy, my voice weak.

Her reaction at the other hip is just as gratifying.

Then I slide my hand between her legs and she's so damn wet, my cock jumps in anticipation. I slide her hips forward until she leans back on her elbows.

"I need you," I growl, unbuttoning my jeans.

"I'm yours."

chapter seventeen

Maggie

HE STROKES his thumb down my neck and back up, and it's the inno-cence of the gesture that makes it so erotic. "You're so blasé about sex, so matter-of-fact, but it's an act. You hide behind blowjobs and hot, frantic fucking."

"There's nothing wrong with those things."

His lips quirk. "Agreed." He lowers his mouth to mine and his lips are so close.

I want him to kiss me. I need him to kiss me. I need him to need me. To use me.

His fingers skim up my arms, sending delicious chills through me before they skim down my body and settle on my hips. "Let me touch you," he whispers. "Let me break down these walls you keep hiding be-hind."

He's so close, leaning over me, his mouth above mine, but I'm pretty sure I'm shaking. How does he see me when no one else has? How does he know?

When he kisses me, his lips aren't gentle. His mouth is hard and hot and demanding over mine. His tongue invades and his teeth scrape my lips. This isn't a kiss, this is a claiming. And it terrifies and exhilarates me.

His hands squeeze roughly at my ass as he settles me on the edge of the table, his mouth still on mine. The cool air is almost painful against my heated skin, but it's a good kind of pain. I'm feeling. I'm present. I'm alive.

I reach for him, my hand trailing down the hard planes of his chest and below, but he clasps my wrist before I can take him in my hand.

"Let *me*," he growls, trapping my hands under his.

His mouth trails down my neck and between my breasts. He presses his tongue to my navel and licks a trail back up to the pulse at the hollow of my neck. I am exposed and arousal pools between my legs, winds tight and achy and wonderful there.

When I lean my head back and close my eyes, I feel his breath at my ear. "Open them. Watch me."

So I do. He dips his mouth to one breast and then the other, drawing my nipples impossibly tight. Then he sinks lower and opens his mouth against my belly. He hooks his hands behind my knees, the muscles in his shoulders bunching as he lifts them, bending my legs out until they're settled against me on the edge and I am completely and intimately open and exposed to him.

My breath is short and shallow, matching the rapid rise and fall of his chest as he pauses to look. When his eyes on me, on that most private part of me, are too much, I press my knees together. He stops me with the press of his thumbs into my inner thighs.

"You're beautiful," he whispers, finally lifting his eyes to mine. "So beautiful that I won't let you hide yourself from me." He lowers his head and blows a cool stream of air against my exposed sex.

A cry slips from my lips.

"Let me kiss you here. Let go for me."

"Asher," I whisper. His mouth is so close and my body is humming, aching.

He lowers his head and puts his mouth on me. His breath, his lips, his tongue, his teeth, on and against me. And this feels so good, so amazing. The sight of his dark head between my legs, the way his muscles bunch as if his control is this heavy load he must strain against. I watch, and I feel, and I sink into the pleasure of his mouth working and teasing and exploring.

At some point, he releases one of my legs and slides two fingers deep inside me while his mouth closes over my clit. I think I scream and I lift my hips, rocking into his fingers and mouth. His fingers curl roughly against my thigh and he shifts my knee further back, opening me to his fingers and mouth somehow deeper still. And I shatter, my sex pulsing around his fingers, swollen and spent against his mouth.

I've hardly recovered when he's standing, toppling the chair in his haste. He sheaths himself in a condom and slides into me.

Hands holding tight to my hips, Asher locks eyes with me as I rock into him. I want to close my eyes—wash away in the feel of his thickness invading my tender sex—but I keep them open. For him. For me.

Asher

She answers the door in a fluffy pink robe and a smile. "You're early," she says, but judging by the way her eyes skim over my body, she's not disappointed to see me.

I couldn't convince her to stay over last night. She had plenty of excuses, wanting to be at the gallery early in the morning, not wanting to leave her dog alone another night. Ultimately, I decided not to push it.

She backs into the house and waves me in. "I'll be ready in ten minutes. Make yourself comfortable."

As she retreats to the bathroom, I give a few seconds of consideration to following her, untying the robe and pulling it from her shoulders, but I dismiss the idea. I promised her I'd take her into Chicago to visit some art gallery today. When I get her naked again, I'm going to need more than a few stolen minutes, so I settle into a chair and look around.

I want to get Maggie out of this crappy little house. Before this year, I hadn't spent much time in New Hope, but even I know this is an unsavory area more known for meth dealing than the neighborhood watch.

I could put her up in a nice apartment by campus, but she's so drawn to the river, I think she'd be happier at my place by the water.

Who am I kidding? I want her close. After my probation ends, I'm planning on spending a month in New York talking to studios for the first time since Infinite Gray broke up, and I want to know she's waiting for me when I get back.

My thoughts stutter to a halt when she returns to the living room.

"Jesus Christ." I stand and step closer to get a better look. She's in red. A flowing little sleeveless thing that shows just enough cleavage and a whole lot of leg. Her hair is pinned up off her neck, but a few little tendrils hang loose. My eyes trail down to her strappy heels and I'm struck with an image of stripping her down to nothing but her shoes.

Oh, hell yes.

When I return to her face, her cheeks are tinged pink. "I guess I don't need to ask how I look."

Closing the steps between us, I pull her into my arms and press my face into the crook of her neck—to taste her skin, to take a hit of her scent. "How am I supposed to look at you all day and not touch you?" I growl into her soft skin.

My hand slips under her dress almost of its own volition, and I trail my fingers up her thighs.

"Who said you couldn't touch me?" Her breathing is already uneven as I trace the lace of her panties over her hip to the small of her back.

I slap her ass softly. "Don't tempt me."

I don't understand the tension in Maggie's shoulders. I would expect her to feel at home in a gallery like this.

The space is large, with high ceilings and track lighting that illuminates the artwork.

A man wanders from the back to greet us, and he takes one look at my tattoos and earrings and dismisses me. Never mind that there isn't piece in here I can't afford. *Asshole.*

"I'm Martin, the gallery manager. Are we just here to peruse?" But then he looks at Maggie and does a double-take, eyes widening.

Maggie doesn't seem to notice. She extends her hand and flashes him that gorgeous smile. "Hello, I'm Maggie and this is Asher. We understand you have some Bauer paintings on display here?"

I thought we were here to check out the gallery. I didn't realize she was looking for a specific artist.

The man's expression is different when he looks at me this time. Being here with Maggie has clearly earned me some sort of art-world street cred. "Of course, yes." He offers me his hand. "It's such an honor. Let me show you to the back."

He scurries ahead and we hang back. When Maggie turns, I catch her eye and mouth, "Honor?"

She lifts a shoulder and shakes her head, but worry creases her brow and her shoulders stiffen even more. There's something she's not telling me.

We follow the man through the large space, the echo of our steps mingling with the soft piano melody playing through the overhead speakers.

He motions to a doorway off the back. "Mr. Bauer's collection has attracted a lot of attention to the gallery in the past months. Just stunning. You should be very pleased."

I frown and Maggie hugs herself, rubbing her bare arms. Judging by the way she's staring at the door, I'm not sure she's going to enter.

"Shall we?" I say, taking her hand and leading her through the swinging door.

Inside the smaller room is a series of portraits of beautiful women. My eye catches a flash of red in the far corner and I turn to see a portrait of Maggie, her hair lifted by the breeze as she looks at the river. She wears nothing but a thin sheet wrapped under her arms.

Next to me, Maggie's shoulders sag and she starts breathing normally for the first time since we arrived at the gallery.

The studio manager is eyeing her curiously. "Dr. Bauer has such talent. It's true art. Not too sexy. Tasteful." His eyes are on Maggie as he says the last. Those words can't mean much coming from a man who looks at her like he jacks off to the image of her face every night, but I suspect he's nearly as stunned to have her here as I am to see the painting.

"Do we need to go?" I ask softly.

She lifts her chin and smiles at the attendant. "Are these the only paintings of his you have?"

The man frowns. "Yes. Were you looking for something else?"

She shakes her head. "No. You've been helpful, thank you."

I wrap my arm around her waist, half surprised when she doesn't push me away, and we make our way toward the door.

"I'm sorry if that surprised you," the attendant says behind us. "I thought you knew. I thought that was why you came."

"I'm fine." She says, but she doesn't look at him or me as we head to the car. No, all she does is slide her hand into mine and squeeze hard. And it's enough for me.

"Who painted it, Maggie?"

We're at a little coffee shop down the road from the gallery. I offered to take her to a bar—God knows she looks like she could use a drink—but she declined.

So, here we are. Coffee in hand. The silence of unspoken secrets between us.

I need to know about the painting we saw, but more I need to know about the ones we didn't, the ones she is clearly looking for.

"Ethan Bauer," she says. "He's an art professor at Sinclair." Her voice is clear, strong, as if this isn't difficult for her. I don't buy it.

"When did he paint it?"

"A couple of years ago."

The whirring of the steamer rents through the air as the barista fills an order.

When it stops, I say, "You were a student."

Maggie takes a sip from her cup and avoids my eyes. "A lot of students pose and in a lot less than a sheet. Of course, I wasn't a student of *his* at the time, but he was my mentor."

"Your mentor?"

She nods. "I came to Sinclair for painting. Ethan took me under his wing early on. To foster my talent, he said."

"That's why we came up here, isn't it? You wanted to see if he was showing a painting of you?" I pause for a beat. "You were relieved when you saw it. What did you expect to see?"

She studies her coffee, buying time, and I expect her to dodge the question. I'm surprised when she says, "Ethan painted a whole series of me. A semi-erotic collection of paintings he swore he'd never show."

"And you're afraid he will."

"We had an affair." The words are so soft I almost don't hear them over the soft chatter of the people around us. "He had a bit of a…reputation for sleeping with his models. It wasn't like I didn't know what I was getting myself into." She closes her eyes. "But I don't want anyone seeing those paintings."

"Why the secrecy?"

She's silent so long I don't think she's going to answer. Maggie is such a paradox. On one hand, she's an open book. She doesn't bother disguising the truth when it isn't pretty, and she doesn't seem to be ashamed for her decisions. Except with this area of her life. When it comes to Will, the miscarriage, and the last year, she is closed and impossible to read. She is full of secrets and fighting like hell to protect them.

"You had an affair with him, but you were marrying Will."

Her eyes snap open. "I never slept with Ethan when I was engaged to Will. I may have done a lot of things wrong that year, but once Will and I were involved, things between Ethan and me were over." She lowers her voice and traces a scar in the oak tabletop. "Will deserved at least that much from me."

"What happened to end things between you and Ethan?"

"Ethan was married." She avoids my eyes. "I just woke up. I realized I had fallen into the same patterns as I had in high school. Maybe the sex was consensual this time, but it still wasn't healthy. He was married. He was never going to leave his wife."

"And you were pregnant," I say softly.

Her wild eyes shoot to mine so quickly, I know I'm right. The married man knocked Maggie up, and she hurried and got engaged to an eligible young guy who could play daddy.

Her shoulders rise and fall with her deep breath. She won't look at me.

"Maggie," I say softly.

"I know it sounds stupid coming from someone who had sex with a married man, but I didn't want to hurt anyone."

She chews on the edge of her lip, and I find myself wanting to cup her face in my hands and kiss that abused spot, kiss across her cheeks and down her neck, kiss away the pain and the self-loathing.

She looks like she survived a natural disaster. Worry and concern distort her features.

I try to imagine what that was like for her. Finding herself pregnant with a married man's baby after what happened to her in high school. And I can see it. I can see how a marriage to a willing and available man may have seemed like the answer.

"Would you mind waiting her for a few minutes while I run a quick errand?"

She blinks at me.

"I promise I'll be back in less than twenty minutes."

chapter eighteen

Maggie

I AM quickly coming to believe that there is no place in this world I love as much as Asher's arms, talking about nothing and everything in the darkness.

We didn't say much on the drive home from Chicago. He played some music for me, pointing out influences for his new work and sharing his favorite songs. He didn't ask me any more questions about Ethan or Will. He didn't bring up the baby.

And I didn't ask about the blanket-covered backseat holding something that hadn't been there on the drive up.

When we got home and slipped out of our clothes, I caught myself waiting for Asher to touch me, to seduce me, to use me. Then I remembered this was Asher, and it wasn't like that between us.

"Will you go to the gallery opening with me this weekend?" I ask him quietly now.

"Of course."

I watch his expression in the darkness. "Ethan's holding his cards close to his chest, and he won't tell anyone what he's showing in his part of the exhibit."

"You think he might show the paintings of you?"

"I'm afraid he might," I say softly. "I want to prepare myself for that possibility."

"I'll be by your side," he promises.

Warmth blossoms in my chest. I know I can handle this if Asher is by my side.

"Where did you disappear to last year?" he asks.

My fingertips freeze where they'd been tracing the outline of his tattoo. "What?"

He pushes himself up on an elbow. "Last year, you left after you called off your wedding. Where did you go?"

Don't ruin this. Please, don't. "I wanted to get away for a while. I was…more than a little messed up at the time. I needed to get away."

"From Ethan? From Will? From what happened in high school?"

I sit up. "From everyone. From this town." I command my racing heart to slow. Asher is not the enemy. "Why do you care so much?"

"Why are you still hiding from me?"

"You already know. You know more than anyone." I close my eyes, trying to center myself. "I'm going to go to sleep now. I'm sorry if you want to talk more, but this isn't my idea of fun."

I click off the light and move to the far side of the bed. I'm nude but it's his questions that made me feel naked.

Asher's big arm wraps around me and pulls me against his warm, bare chest. "Is it just me," he whispers, "or do you not trust anyone?"

I think about how much it meant to have him with me at the gallery this morning, how he was the only one I could ask to go with me to find the Discovery collection, how easy it was to answer his questions about Ethan. "I don't trust anyone *but* you Asher, but trusting you scares me more than you can understand. I'm fighting it every day."

"Don't shut me out anymore." He kisses my shoulder. "Let me in."

"No one knows about Ethan," I say softly. "It took my family years to recover from the scandal with Toby. This is a small town. People here are cruel and their memories are long. I couldn't tell my mother I was pregnant with a married man's baby. Not after what I put her through in high school."

He presses his lips to my shoulder. "I understand that. And obviously Will did too if he was willing to play along."

I stiffen in his arms, and my heart pounds painfully in my chest until I hear the whoosh of his exhale.

"Will knew the baby wasn't his, right?"

I close my eyes.

Everything had happened so fast. I panicked. It seemed like one minute I'd been hovering in post-coital bliss, running my fingertips through the soft sprinkle of hair on Ethan's chest, and the next I'd been falling hard for Will.

I remember that last morning with Ethan. His studio smelled of sex and stale wine and the sun poked its golden head in between the curtains.

He grabbed my hand, pressed his lips against my palm. "I wish I could stay here with you all weekend, Margaret, but Claudia is going to kill me as it is."

"What will you tell her?" I asked as I explored his body with my fingertips.

"The truth."

"Really?"

"I will tell her that I was working in my studio and fell asleep." He turned, shifting his body so he was on his side, facing me. "I wish I could give you more, Maggie. You deserve more than a bum who's sneaking around on his wife."

"I've never asked for more," I whispered, and it was true. "But I wonder sometimes…" I wasn't sure I could say it.

"About what?" He was already moving, pulling himself off our makeshift bed of sheets and pillows on the studio floor and reaching for his paint-stained jeans.

"What would you do if something happened? If…I don't know. If I got pregnant or something."

His hands froze where they'd been working his fly. "We've always used protection."

I rolled to sitting and crossed my feet under me. "Nothing's one hundred percent," I told the floor. If anyone knew that, it was me. I heard it over and over again from my mother. At my Catholic high school, there'd been no sex talk beyond a brief statement that sex was something sacred that should be preserved for marriage, that contraception was against God's will, and that no contraceptive method was one hundred percent effective. If young women wanted to really protect themselves and please God, they needed to do so with chastity.

"Are you trying to tell me something?" His voice was so cautious, his face so guarded that I felt foolish. It was the first time he made me feel like a kid. But I had to know.

"Hypothetically." This wasn't me. Skirting the issue. Guarding the truth.

"Maggie, I know it takes two. I'd take care of you."

The world contained so much hope at that moment. So much it had poured into me, like the early morning sunshine that warmed the studio.

I raised my eyes to meet his, that golden sunshine filling my most dark and desperate corners. I hadn't taken a test yet, but my period was nine days late and I was like clockwork. My supply of denial was running dry.

"I know you couldn't afford to take care of it yourself," he explained. "I'd take you to Indy or Chicago. We'd get it taken care of there. Discreetly. And I'd pay for it. You don't need to worry about that."

Get it taken care of?

Even now, my hand clutches my stomach instinctively, as if the threat still looms. The golden warmth fled and red-hot terror replaced it.

I remember ignoring his hand and pushing myself up off the floor. The gesture had felt meaningful, and I told myself that it had only been a matter of time before our relationship came to its inevitable end.

I grabbed my jeans and sweater, trying to keep my movements slow and natural—and fearing I was failing. "You better get home to Claudia."

His fingertips grazed the small of my back as I bent to pull on my jeans. For the first time, they weren't a lover's fingertips. They were the enemy's. For the first time, the touch of this married man, my mentor, my professor, made me feel unclean to the core.

I ended our affair that morning. I told him I wanted more from life than to be his mistress. It was so true. I wanted so much more from *him*. But he couldn't give it. And at that moment, as I stood in the soft trickle of morning light and ached inside with a betrayal that cut to the very foundation of my beliefs, I knew I'd never ask him to give me anything else. Not ever again.

Asher brings me back to the present with his lips on my shoulder. "Tell me," he says softly.

"The day I told Will I was pregnant, I was planning on telling him the truth. But he…" I trail off, sickened by my own lies. "He assumed it was his and I let him."

"He deserves to know," he says softly, and I hear something like pain in his voice. "Despite…everything."

"I know."

The garage is dark, save for the glow of the Jeep's dome light. The concrete floor is cold under my feet.

I move the blanket from the backseat, and my throat grows thick at the sight of the framed canvas. I know he bought it for me.

I stand frozen, hypnotized by that goddamned painting.

There's nothing scandalous about this one, but he bought it. For me.

I hope I deserve him.

I head back into the house and to the couch in the great room. My gaze drifts to the staircase. I should go back to bed. It would be so nice, curling up with a man who wants to protect me, letting him hold me, hiding inside his warmth. Maybe I could even wake him and tell him my story, explain how I let things get out of control. I made mistakes, and I tried to make amends for those mistakes.

Maybe Asher would listen. Maybe if I shattered, he *would* find me.

My hand curls at my stomach.

I didn't give my baby away because I suddenly became a noble woman who couldn't live with a lie. I gave her away because, in the gritty ultrasound image, I saw the blinking beat of my daughter's heart, and I already loved her too much to make *her* live with it.

All week, I've felt something tugging inside me. Like a hidden ribbon unraveling and exposing what I've so carefully kept tucked away.

I want to tell Asher about Grace, but I'm terrified he won't understand.

It *would* feel so nice to have someone on my side. To have a little help carrying the weight of my secrets. And I want to tell someone. I want to utter her name just once. Let just one other living soul in on the secret—screw-up Maggie Thompson created something beautiful.

Asher

She's sleeping on my couch with her arms wrapped around herself. She looks so damn lonely it breaks my heart.

"Asher?" She blinks up at me as I lift her into my arms. "What are you doing?"

"I'm taking you back to bed. I can't sleep for shit without you next to me." My jaw tightens against the words. I don't like to think about how much I need this woman. I don't like that, while I need her more every day, she's still pushing me away.

Even as I think it, she wraps her arms around my neck and leans her head against my chest. "Thank you," she whispers. "I forget that I don't have to be alone when you're around."

My heart squeezes, and I take the stairs two at a time. When I reach my bedroom, I don't take her to the bed. Instead, I carry her into the bathroom and lower her onto the edge of the jetted tub while I run the water.

As it fills, I strip off my underwear and help her out of her clothes. She gives me a soft smile and lifts her arms over her head so I can remove the t-shirt. Then she stands and I take my time sliding my hands under the soft, thin cotton of her panties. Dropping to my knees on the heated tile, I take them over her hips slowly. When she's completely bare, I kiss her foot, inside at the arch, the soft curve of her calf and the hot flesh of her inner thigh. Then I hover at the apex of her thighs, a breath away from tasting her.

"You're so gorgeous."

"I like the look of you like that," she tells me with a grin. "On your knees like you're worshipping me."

I lift my gaze to meet hers. "You have no idea."

Standing, I skim my fingers over her. Hips, waist, and breasts that I will never tire of touching.

Then I take her hand and lead her into the tub, settling her between my legs so I can hold her in my arms where she belongs. The hot water pulses around us, and she relaxes into me as I trace an invisible path from her breasts to her hipbone.

"You're the first man I've ever been with that doesn't want to have sex every time we're naked."

I press my lips to her neck, scrape my teeth over the shell of her ear. "There's more to intimacy than fucking," I whisper, sliding my hand between her legs.

I love the sound of her gasp as my fingers slip over her clit, savor the tilt of her hips as my palm settles against her.

"You are so beautiful. I could spend hours touching you."

She draws in a breath as I lift my hand from between her legs and return to tracing lazy paths across her abdomen.

"Are you going to tell me about this?" I rest my fingers over the silvery stretch marks at her navel.

She sighs, but she doesn't tense. She relaxes into me further. "You already know." The relief is in her voice.

"Zoe's mother developed the same thing after her pregnancy. I didn't put it together at first, but today..." I trail off. There's no reason to say more.

"They're my favorite part of my body," she whispers, sliding her fingers between mine. "Because they're proof she was mine once."

My heart squeezes painfully. Juliana had cursed her stretch marks, had hated the way pregnancy changed her body. Maggie is so miraculously different, I want to breathe her in.

"I thought you had a miscarriage." I brush her hair over her shoulder. "That day at the river?"

"A blood clot," she says softly. "I had to believe I was losing her before I could accept that I had to give her up."

"It was a girl?"

She sniffs and leans her head into the crook of my shoulder. "They named her Grace."

I close my eyes, trying to imagine what it must have been like for her.

"I wanted to keep her, but I couldn't do that to my mom. So when Will assumed the baby was his and asked me to marry him..." She releases a long, slow breath.

"Did you ever tell Ethan?"

"He wanted me to get an abortion. I just...I couldn't."

"You did a beautiful thing." I wrap my arms around her waist and squeeze. "You are so amazing."

Maggie

Asher's sleeping and the steady rhythm of his breathing has me drifting off.

When I came back to New Hope, I imagined a lonely life of grief and secrets, and life stretched out before me like a threat.

I know they think I tried to kill myself the morning I had the accident in my studio, but I hadn't. But when I saw the blood pool at my feet, I hadn't been scared. I'd been grateful that maybe it was over, maybe I wouldn't have to do this anymore.

Asher changed that, and now life stretches before me full of hope and possibility.

I press my lips against his bare shoulder. I close my eyes and feel sleep wrapping me in its cottony grasp.

"I love you," I whisper to this sleeping man. "Thank you for finding me."

He surprises me by rolling to face me and drawing me against his chest. "I love you too."

chapter nineteen

Maggie

"I'M GLAD you finally took me up on my offer," Ethan says, sliding into the booth across from me.

The upscale Indianapolis restaurant he chose is clattering with the bustle of a healthy weeknight dinner crowd.

Sighing, I look at my watch. He's fifteen minutes late. Some things never change.

He reaches across the table, brushing my hand with his. "How are you, Maggie?"

I pull away. "I'm not here because I want to reconnect."

"That's a shame, though I can't say I'm surprised. I always figured you'd move on to bigger and better things than a small-town art professor. Who is the lucky guy? That rock star fellow, right? Much more your speed, I imagine."

I shake my head. Why hadn't I seen his constant manipulation for what it was from the beginning? "I don't want to talk about my private life. I want to know what you're doing with the Discovery collection. I deserve to know."

He stills and jaw tightens. "Why?"

"Do you really want Claudia to find out about us?" I ask softly. "Those paintings will give you away."

"I'm an artist," he says. "She knows that."

"Ethan, I was pregnant when I left you."

He doesn't move, doesn't offer any response, aside from cutting his eyes to the menu.

"I was pregnant with your baby when I became engaged to Will."

Still no response. I want to smack him.

"But I couldn't go through with it." I'm surprised how easily the words come. "I couldn't go through with the lie, so I called off the wedding and moved to Connecticut where I lived in a maternity group home until the baby was born."

He places his napkin in his lap and lifts a hand to signal the server. "Do you have any wine by the glass?"

"Yes, sir," the server says, producing a leather-bound menu.

Ethan studies it for a moment before pointing to his selection. "Two glasses, please."

"Excellent choice. I'll be right back with that, sir."

I wait, determined to give him time to soak in my confession. He doesn't speak until after the server arrives with the wine and leaves again.

Ethan takes a tentative sip. "It has a lovely, earthy flavor."

My patience snaps. "Do you understand what I'm telling you? I had your baby and gave her up for adoption."

His gaze narrows. "I understood the first time, but thank you for the translation."

"I don't want you trying to contact her," I explain. "She has a good life with a good family, and I won't have you destroying that."

He slams his wine down, making the red contents slosh to the rim. "What, exactly, makes you think that I want anything to do with the child that you allege is mine?"

Fury whips through me. "I don't *allege* anything—"

"Listen, Margaret. I didn't want anything to do with the child when you practically confessed your pregnancy in my studio last year, and I certainly don't want anything to do with it now. Even if it was, as you suggest, my own, it wasn't the product of my intentions."

"Wasn't the *product* of your *intentions*?" The pressure inside me is too much. I want to strangle the bastard. "She's a child, not a *painting*. And what do you—" My breath catches as his full meaning hits me. I'm so angry I hadn't fully registered his words. "You knew?"

He rolls a starched white sleeve and opens his menu. "Contrary to what you seem to think of me, I'm not dense. I knew. I even knew that you gave it up for adoption, though that took a bit more digging. It was in my best interest to know that you weren't going to try anything ridiculous like raising the child on your own."

Flames of anger twisted inside me. "Why would that have been ridiculous?" I have to ask because it's the question that won't leave me alone. Why *would* it have been so ridiculous? Why couldn't I have been a single mom? I could have done it. The truth would have hurt my mother but she would have survived.

Ethan glances up from the menu and smiles sweetly. "Because I didn't need you coming around asking for child support years down the road." He shrugs. "Like I said, I have no reason to believe it was mine. If you'll remember, chastity has never been a virtue of yours."

I force myself to swallow my rage, but it goes down chalky and bitter. "I'm leaving."

"Suit yourself."

I stop, take a breath, and turn slowly. "I sacrificed everything to keep this secret. If you show those paintings, it's hard to say how much of that is going to be brought out into the open."

"Are you worried the truth might ruin things with your latest boy toy? Don't fool yourself, Margaret."

"Some of us are just too cold inside to be capable of real love." He doesn't say the words now, but he doesn't need to. He said them enough in the past that they hang in the air between us.

I used to believe those words, but I don't anymore.

William

I've lost her. I can see it in her eyes. She stands taller somehow, and even when she's not smiling she looks happy. I'm grateful for that, but jealous as hell I couldn't be the one to do that for her.

The gallery gleams. Everything is ready to go for tomorrow night's opening, save the Bauer exhibition in the side room.

Even though she's glowing and standing taller, I can tell Ethan's missing pieces have Maggie worried.

"Did he give you any hint about it?" I ask her when I catch her staring into the empty space.

She swallows and shakes her head.

"He painted a lot of women, Maggie. I'm sure no one will know about the affair if he shows paintings of you."

She doesn't respond, but eventually she turns to me, arms wrapped around herself. "If you knew about the affair, why didn't you ever question whose baby it was?" Her face is lined with grief I wish I could take away.

"You know one of the reasons Krystal and I were such a good match?" I ask, answering her question with one of my own. "She doesn't mind adopting."

Maggie blinks at me. "Adopting?"

"Yeah. We were going to make our family that way." I wait a beat. "I'm sterile. I found out when I was sixteen. Football accident." I wince. "Cleats aren't very forgiving."

"Sixteen?" she whispers. I can practically see her mind piecing together the implications of my confession.

"I would have taken you however I could get you, Maggie." I shove my hands in my pockets. "I still would. I don't think you ever understood that. I don't think you ever believed you were worthy of that kind of love."

Maggie

He never asked me if the baby was his. I always wondered at that kind of trust. I pegged it for naiveté. I said I was pregnant and he asked me to marry him.

But Will knew he was sterile. Which meant he had known the baby couldn't be his. He knew I was asking him to raise another man's child.

And he hadn't said a word because he'd thought that was what I wanted.

"I need to sit down," I say softly.

I head for the patio and Will follows me out. We settle into seats at the stone table, breathing in the fresh evening air.

"I should have told you," he says. "If you'd known I knew the truth, you might not have hated yourself so much."

I look into his baby blues and see honesty there. "You were trying to protect me."

"I'd do anything for you, Maggie." He draws in a shaky breath. "I should have waited for you. I would have if I'd believed—"

"It wouldn't have made a difference." I have to cut him off. I can't make him suffer like this. "Don't beat yourself up for falling for Krystal. I'd already ruined what we had by lying."

He's watching me, pain in those beautiful eyes. "I don't suppose I could talk you into starting over. Starting fresh. With me."

My breath snags on the edge of my healing heart. "I'm in love with Asher."

He closes his eyes as if he can't stand to see my words hit the air. As if looking at me while I say them makes them too real.

"You're going to find someone, Will. I know you're going to get your happily-ever-after."

"And you're sure he can give you yours?"

"I don't think you ever believed you were worthy of that kind of love."

I hadn't believed. Until Asher.

"I'm sure."

chapter twenty

Maggie

"HERE'S TO a new home for martini nights!" Hanna says, lifting her margarita glass.

I grin and take a swig of my beer. I don't know what it is about Brady's—the memories, the neon Bud signs, the clack of billiard balls in the background—but I love being here. "Thanks for meeting me," I say to my sisters. "Tomorrow's the gallery opening, and I wanted to celebrate."

"I can't wait," Lizzy says. "I bought a new little black dress and red heels that make me horny just lookin' at 'em."

The front door opens and Kenny strolls in. It's late on a Friday, and, judging by the way he's walking, he might already be a little drunk. "Lucy!" he hoots when he spots me.

"Get a life," Hanna growls.

He stumbles toward our table. "I'm not hurting anyone."

"I need to visit the little girls' room," I announce, ignoring Kenny. "Either of you want to join me?"

"I'm not ready to break the seal," Hanna says. "I'm going to get us another round. Want another?"

I look at my half-full beer and shake my head. "No. I'm good."

A little bit of a crowd has formed, townies taking advantage of a beautiful June night free of college kids, and I have to maneuver through the crowd to reach the bathroom.

When I see my reflection in the mirror, I almost don't recognize myself. I look...lighter. Happier. It's been a summer, but worth it.

When I come back out into the dark hallway, Kenny's waiting on the other side of the door.

He doesn't let me get far before he has me in the corner, body pressed against mine, hands against the wall on either side of my head.

"Hey, Maggie," he says softly, his eyes on my mouth.

I know I'm in trouble when I hear him use my real name, and I swallow the bile rising in my throat. When the boys at my high school decided I was a slut, I learned quickly they thought this meant I existed for their pleasure, to use when and how they pleased. For a while, I believed them.

Fuck that.

"Kenny, you're drunk. Back off."

He leans closer and my nose is greeted with the scent of beer and onion rings. "Nah," he says, "that's not what you want."

His thumb grazes the edge of my jaw and I struggle to keep my cool, not to panic. I'll get rid of him. He's just a stupid asshole looking for an easy lay, but he's looking with the wrong girl.

"Kenny, you don't want this. What would your wife think?"

"But that's what you like, isn't it? Fucking married men?" His lips curl into a twisted smile. "You act like you've changed, but I know you get around."

I snarl. "You don't know shit."

"Admit it. You're a little wet thinking about me fucking you against this wall and then going home to my wife. You like being the pussy we dream about when we go to bed with our sexless wives."

The moment his hand slides between my legs, I bring my knee to his groin. But I didn't give Kenny enough credit. He presses closer, stealing my leverage at the last minute. His sweaty hand grabs at my inner thigh and I try again, using the very little room I have to draw up hard with my knee.

At first I think I hit him with more power than I have because he flies off me and slams against the opposite wall.

Then I see Asher, fists clenched and eyes blazing as he bears down on Kenny.

"What the *fuck*, man?" Kenny whimpers. "Get your own bitch."

"She told you to *back off*," Asher growls.

"And who are you? Pussy patrol?"

The sick crunch of knuckles connecting with jawbone echoes in the small corridor.

People are gathering at the end of the hall, attracted by the shouts and the familiar sounds of a bar scuffle.

Kenny sneers, his lip bloody. "You can have the cunt," he grumbles. "She was asking for it, but a dick's a dick to her. Mine? Yours? What's it matter?"

Asher's nostrils flare. As I step forward to stop him, he sweeps Kenny's legs out from under him, taking him down.

"Asher," I cry, but he doesn't hear me.

Asher's on the floor, leaning over Kenny when Will appears in the throng and pulls him off.

Asher's eyes blaze as he rounds on Will.

"Let it go, man," Will says. "He's not worth it."

Kenny pushes himself up on his elbows and moans. His lip is bleeding and his right eye is already swelling. His buddy Craig helps him off the floor, glaring at me the whole time. "Why are you getting messed up with Lucy anyway?"

Asher jumps forward at those words, but not before Will can wrap an arm around his waist and hold him back.

I have become that helpless woman who can do nothing but stare as the world moves around her, and before I know it, the police are there, and I want to cry because I recognize both of the uniformed officers who come into Brady's. They both went to my high school. They're both lifelong "bros" with Kenny, and they don't ask a single question before they take Asher to the back of a patrol car.

"Wait!" I call, my voice weak. "He was protecting me!"

"We're just taking him in for questioning," one officer promises, but I fucking know this town and I know how the good ole boy system works. Asher won't get to say his piece. They'll hold him as long as they can and record whatever story makes Kenny look the best.

"I was on my way to take a piss," Kenny's saying, "and she kinda pushes me against the wall and presses her hand to my crotch."

My jaw drops. The officer is jotting down notes as if Kenny's story is more than a load of bullshit, and I can't find my tongue.

"I should have pushed her off. I should have, but I've been drinking and I guess I let my dick think for me. Next thing I know her boyfriend's throwing punches right and left, throwing me against the wall and slamming my head against the floor." He wipes the blood from his nose with the back of his hand and a waitress hurries over with a napkin. "I didn't know she had a boyfriend and didn't think to worry about it. I wasn't thinking at all, honestly."

"You weren't thinking because you were too busy trying to force your hand up my skirt to listen to me say *no*, let alone *think*."

"Everyone knows Asher Logan's a hot head," Kenny's buddy says, crossing his arms. "Only reason he's even in this town is so he can stay out of trouble while he serves his probation."

"No. He was protecting me. Asher didn't do anything wrong." My voice trills with the panic that's weighing heavier and heavier on me. My lungs are shrinking and I can't get the air I need.

"Who are the police gonna believe?" Craig mutters in my ear. "Their life-long friend or the slut with a track record for fucking married men?"

I can't breathe. There's no air back here. "Get *away* from me," I scream, pushing at Craig because I know what happens next, I know what this means for Asher.

"Maggie!" Hanna and Lizzy appear at the edge of the throng and push their way back to me.

"We'll need to talk to her," an officer says without looking up from his notes. Kenny's still waxing redneck poetic about my hallway seduction. I have no doubt his wife will know about this before the night's out. Just another person who hates me in this town and for once I don't give a shit what they think. But Asher…

"Maggie," Hanna is saying, "breathe, sweetie."

"She needs air," Lizzy announces, clearing a path through the crowd. For the officers, she tosses back, "We'll be outside when you're ready to talk to us."

"What the hell happened?" Lizzy asks as we push through the front doors.

"Hush," Hanna barks. "Can't you see she's in shock?" She settles me onto a concrete bench in front of the bar and takes my face in both her hands. "Breathe."

"I'm fine," I object. But I'm not fine. I haven't been fine since I was a little girl, since before my body turned on me and ruined my life. I focus on my breathing, expanding my belly until it hurts and exhaling slowly. "I need my purse."

Lizzy hands it over, and I dig out my anxiety medication and pop one in my mouth.

"What's that?" Hanna asks softly, taking the bottle from me. "Jesus, how long have you needed this?"

I blink at her. How long have I needed it or how long have I been taking it?

"I can't believe what they're trying to say about you," Hanna says. "As if that was *your* fault?"

They can't hurt me. They don't matter. I am not the sum of their accusations.

The mantras from my therapist do nothing to soothe my panic when this isn't about me. It's about the man who probably just lost everything protecting me.

"Oh." Hanna pops up and shoves the bottle in her pocket. "Hi, Will."

Will stands a couple of yards from me, his broad shoulders silhouetted by the street lamp and his face masked in shadow.

"Are you okay?" he asks me softly, running a hand through his hair.

I nod. "Kenny didn't hurt me. He didn't get a chance."

"They'll probably keep Asher overnight. There'll be an arraignment in the morning and the judge will set bail. Kenny doesn't need medical attention, so it shouldn't be a big deal. A fine, maybe? It's going to be okay, Maggie."

I swallow hard. *My. Fault.* "He's on probation. He can't have any charges brought against him or he'll lose his daughter. He'll have to serve that old sentence for assault." I'm shaking. "He'll go to prison."

"Shit," Will mutters.

"But who gets to decide?" Hanna pipes in. "Who listens to everyone's side and decides if they should even press charges?"

"If it's the goddamned cops in this town, Asher is screwed," Lizzy says.

I wince and Hanna says, "Liz!"

"The police don't make that call," Will says.

We all look at him, waiting, until I realize what he's not saying.

179

"The prosecutor," I whisper.

"Oh, no," Hanna cries.

"He's an outsider, Mags," Will says, jaw hard. "This doesn't look good."

Lizzy props her hands on her hips. "I'm so damn sick of this backwards town."

I don't reply because out of the corner of my eye, I see the flashing lights of the patrol car edging around the corner. I stand and let my fingers slide against the glass of the back door as it passes as a crawl.

Asher's head is inclined against the back of the seat, and he winks at me and flashes me a sad smile.

My phone buzzes in my pocket, alerting me to a text. From Asher. They must not have taken away Asher's phone yet.

I love you. No regrets.

I lift my eyes to his as the car pulls onto Main Street, and I watch as the lights fade into the darkness.

"He was just protecting me." But if the prosecutor gets to decide whether to press charges, protecting me may be the worst thing he could have done.

I haven't talked to her since I was fifteen and she was divorcing her husband for sleeping with me.

"Do you want me to go with you?"

I grab a mug and fill it with coffee, shaking my head at Krystal. "I want to go alone." It's barely seven-thirty in the morning, but I'm going to be at the courthouse when the doors open. When I went to the station to give my statement last night, they confirmed what Will had guessed. Asher would be held overnight and bail would be set at the arraignment in the morning.

My stomach churns with anxiety over the price Asher might have to pay for doing the right thing.

"You don't have to do everything alone, you know," Krystal says softly.

Purse halfway to my shoulder, I pause and turn to my sister. I set down my purse, settle my mug and my keys next to it and wrap my arms around her. "I know that now."

She squeezes me hard. "Okay."

I pull into the lot behind the courthouse and cut the ignition by 7:43.

Last night was miserable, giving my statement to those men, knowing they didn't believe me. Knowing they wouldn't care even if they had believed. But I survived it.

I take a last swig of coffee and step out of my car.

"Maggie?"

I turn at the sound of Ann Quimby's voice. "Ms. Quimby."

She's dressed in a smart blue skirt suit and holding a briefcase and looks every bit like a prosecutor should. She narrows her eyes at me. "What are you doing here?"

"I…Asher Logan…last night…" I stutter. I always liked Anna and seeing her again would be awkward under any circumstances, but is especially so under these.

She shakes her head. "Mr. Logan was released this morning."

"Released?"

"I'm not pressing charges. Between your story and Kenny's track record, I have enough reason to believe Mr. Logan used justifiable force to protect you."

My jaw goes slack. "But…Kenny said…" Oh, what I would give for the ability to construct a complete sentence. "Thank you," I whisper.

"You can file a protective order against Kenny," she informs me. "I know Brady doesn't want him in his bar anymore, so you won't have to worry about seeing him there."

I nod. "I will. Thank you."

She turns toward the courthouse.

"Ms. Quimby?" I call.

She stops and turns back to me.

"You don't know how much this means."

She nods. "I'm not in the business of blaming the victim, Miss Thompson." She cuts her eyes away from me and sets her jaw. "I never have been."

We both know she's not just talking about Asher's case.

chapter twenty-one

Asher

WHEN MAGGIE pulls into my driveway, I run outside and pull her against me. She wraps her arms around my neck and cries.

"It's okay, baby," I murmur, stroking her hair. "I've got you."

"I thought they were going to send you to prison," she whispers. "You would have missed a whole year of Zoe's life, and it would have been my fault."

"No." I pull back and hold her face in my hands. "Not your fault. You understand? You didn't ask for Kenny to do that to you."

"But Asher, they could have—"

"I won't let you blame yourself for what some asshole did, Maggie." I kiss her. Hard. When I saw Kenny pushing himself against her last night, I could have killed him. The punches I threw were nothing compared to what I wanted to do.

"I love you," I whisper in her hair.

"I love you too," she whispers back, clinging to me.

Maggie

"Asher?" I call as I step into the house.

We decided to meet here before heading over to the gallery opening, but I decided to come early. If I take my shower and get ready here, that gives Asher and me time alone before we have to leave.

I call for him again as I walk toward the stairs. The house is quiet.

Neither of us slept much last night. Maybe he decided to take a nap.

A smile curves my lips at the thought of Asher laid out across his bed, his broad, bare back exposed, his expression soft in sleep. The thought sends a flutter through my belly, and I toe off my shoes before heading up the stairs. I'm already unbuttoning my jeans, already planning on stripping bare and sliding into bed with him. I'll wrap my arms around him and let the sound of his breathing lull me to sleep.

But when I step into his bedroom, I don't see the darkened space I expect. Instead, I see candlelight and hear the softly thumping beat of the Infinite Gray album.

Licking my lips, I pull my shirt over my head and follow the candlelit path around the corner into the master suite.

I expect to see Asher waiting for me. I expect to see him reading in the chair by the window or sitting in the bed, that wicked smile on his lips. I expect he'll take over for my hands that are currently unbuttoning my pants.

But I don't see Asher at all.

I see a woman on his bed. A long-legged, blond, surgically enhanced, *naked* woman.

My first thought is that I'm in the wrong place. That maybe I somehow walked through the door, up the grand staircase and into the bedroom of the wrong house.

I stutter back a step. The woman's eyes land on me and flash angry, and I know I'm not where I'm supposed to be. There's no mistaking the feminine jealousy flashing across her features, the condescension on her face as she looks me over.

"What do you think *you're* doing here?" she asks with an upturned lip.

She seems totally unconcerned with her nudity, but I have my arms crossed over my bra and I'm backing away instinctively.

"Hey, babe, what's up with all the candles? Trying to burn my house down?"

The woman's eyes widen and her face is like a flower, puckered and closed at the sight of me and now blooming at the sound of his voice.

"I'm in bed, baby," she calls, her calculating eyes never leaving mine. "But you'll need to take out the trash before we can get started."

Asher comes around the corner and freezes when he sees the woman in the bed.

I'm waiting for him to fix this. Waiting for him to ask her what the hell she's doing here. Waiting for him to kick *her* out.

"Juliana." He looks at her, then me, then back to her.

Juliana? His daughter's mother? Are they still together?

"I'm home," the woman says, sweetness dripping from every word. "Aren't you going to give your wife a kiss?"

"Your wife?" Another step back and I knock over a candle. Hot wax splashes onto my bare feet and pools on the shining wood plank floors. "Shit." I hop away from the candle, the wax burning my foot.

"Juliana, get dressed," he growls. Then he turns to me. "I thought we weren't meeting here for another couple hours."

I blink at him. This has to be a dream. Has to be. A horrible nightmare. There's a naked woman in his bed calling herself his wife and he's looking at me like it's my fault because I arrived early?

"You're married?"

"Of course he's married," Juliana says, coming toward us. Her breasts are perky and full and her hip bones protrude on her painfully gaunt frame.

I shake my head. "Is this a joke?" Or a dream. A joke or a dream. But the cooling wax hardening on my foot feels so real, and this would be too cruel a joke from a man I've fallen for.

"Maggie," Asher says softly. "Juliana is Zoe's mom. I told you about her."

"You didn't tell me you were married to her."

His gaze ping pongs between us and his jaw works for a minute before he says, "It's not even a marriage anymore. Just a technicality."

I feel both like I've fallen and jerked to a stop in midair. Now I'm just hanging here, suspended in time. "But you are married."

Juliana wraps her arm around Asher's waist and he pushes it away. "*Clothes,*" he growls.

I can hardly breathe. This is it. This is the proof that I will always be a home-wrecking slut.

I don't know how long I stand there, staring at her as she pulls one of his t-shirts from his drawer like they're her own, staring at him as he repeats, "Listen to me, Maggie."

When Juliana walks back over in the same old band tee I toured this house in last week, I want to vomit. Her arms are crossed under her breasts. "Is she the reason you're leaving me?"

Leaving?

"She's the mother of your child." I'm trying to get this straight, to make sense of it. Oh, God. What have I done?

"We're not together anymore," Asher's saying. "We haven't lived together in over a year. We're getting a divorce."

Juliana sneers at me. "Are you the reason he sent me those divorce papers? Huh? He's leaving me for some teenage country bumpkin?"

I don't tell her I'm not a teenager. I don't tell her I didn't know he was married.

I don't say anything because I've used up all the excuses, and I don't have a single new one worth speaking.

I stagger backward toward the door.

"Don't go, Maggie."

I shake my head. The words "I'm sorry" slip out and I don't even know who I'm apologizing to. Juliana? Asher? Myself?

"I won't let my marriage be ruined by some loose co-ed," Juliana calls. Anger drips from every word. Anger she's entitled to. Anger I deserve.

Asher's calling after me, but I run, and when I hit the stairs I hear him behind me, closer, and run faster. I lose my footing and slide down the last five stairs.

I cry out when I hit the tile floor but I scramble to my feet and reach for the door handle.

"Maggie, don't go, not like this." His hand slams against the door before I can open it. "*Talk* to me."

I force my panicked hands to release the handle and roll my shoulders back. When I turn to him, his face is so close, so agonized, and I hate how much I want to curl into him. I hate how much I want to listen to his explanation. I hate how tempted I am to make excuses. For him. For me.

"I assumed you knew," he says softly.

"Why would I know?" God, it hurts to speak, my throat so thick with jagged bits of my pride. My heart.

"It's never been a secret, Maggie. You never asked and I thought you knew."

"That's not something I should have to ask." My eyes are burning with tears. *Tears.* Fuck him.

"Juliana and I haven't been together in years, but neither one of us was ready to admit it was over." He touches my face. I *let him* touch my face because I am so fucking weak. His thumb tilts up my chin until my eyes meet his. "I was too apathetic to end it. Until you."

A single hot tear rolls down my cheek. "Asher," I say softly.

"Tell me what you need from me, Maggie. You can have it. You know that. *Anything.*"

"I need you to be honest."

"I have *never* lied to you."

"Are you married?"

His face contorts with pain. "Yes, but—"

I put my finger to his lips. "No." I shake my head. "I've heard all the *but's* I can bear. I'm not the gullible child who believes them anymore. I won't be that woman for you. I won't be her for anyone."

"You *aren't* that woman. I'm in love with you. My marriage is over."

"That's what they all say." The laughter that spills from my lips sounds half crazed. "And you know what's so ironic? You're the one who made me give enough of a shit about myself not to believe it anymore."

"Don't lump me in with them." His jaw is hard now. "I'm not like them."

"Let me go, Asher. If you really love me, you won't ask me to stay. You won't make this any harder for me than it already is."

He studies me hard for a moment, as if he could will me to see things his way. Then he drops his hand and steps back, and I rush out the door before I can change my mind.

chapter twenty-two

William

"Jay-sus," Lizzy breathes. "I think everyone in town is here."

The gallery is swarming with locals and out-of-towners, and the crowd spills over onto the patio in the front and the balcony in the back. Wine is flowing, art is selling, and I am fucking miserable.

"You guys should be so damn proud," Lizzy says with a shake of her head.

Krystal's across the room, chatting with Granny, and something tugs long and hard in my chest at the sight of her. We did the right thing. I know we did. But that doesn't keep me from mourning the would-have-beens.

"Oh my God," Lizzy squeaks. "Maggie's here. What the hell happened to her? She looks a mess. Where's Asher? Oh my God, do you think they took him back to prison?"

"No, they didn't press charges."

"But—"

I walk away from Lizzy without excusing myself. Her rapid-fire questions are more than I can bear tonight—even if they're the same questions I have.

Maggie's eyes are puffy and it's obvious she's been crying.

I weave through the crowd and have nearly reached her when Ethan Bauer's assistant squeezes my arm.

"We're ready," she says reverently.

I shift uncomfortably. The side room holding Ethan's top secret collection has been locked up tight since his assistants came to stage it this morning. They insisted the room stay closed until a crowd had gathered.

I nod and the woman scurries over to the steps. "If I could have everyone's attention, we will now open the south room, which features a collection from the illustrious Ethan Bauer."

The crowd applauds and I continue to work my way toward Maggie, who looks lost.

"I present to you," the woman says, "the Discovery collection."

Maggie's head snaps up, and she mouths "No" as the doors open and the crowd files in, their murmurs carrying back into the main room.

I finally reach Maggie's side and she's staring toward the newly opened double doors, her eyes wide. "What is it?" I ask softly. "Are they paintings of you? It's okay, Maggie. No one will know."

She doesn't answer. Instead she says, "Asher is married," and my breath leaves me in a rush. Her eyes meet mine, red-rimmed and vacant. "You knew, didn't you? That's why you said he was just using me for sex."

I swallow and lift a shoulder. "I don't keep up with celebrity gossip, but I knew he used to be. That actress, right? Juliana Weisnith?"

"Yeah. Juliana," she says softly. "God. I trusted him. You're right. I always give myself to the wrong guys. Maybe my dad was right about me. Look at everything I've destroyed."

"No." I take her hand and squeeze. "Don't say that. Your dad didn't even mean the things he said at the end, Maggie. He just...he lost his best friend and his baby girl in one fell swoop, and he said terrible things to try to cope."

She blinks at me and the crowd mills around us, sneaking glances Maggie's way that tell me all I need to know about the paintings in that room.

She cuts her eyes to the doors and back to me. "Will you go in with me?"

I give another squeeze to her hand. "Of course. I'll be right by your side."

The crowd seems to part as we make our way through the doors, and the moment I step inside, I understand, and my feet freeze beneath me. "My God."

The room features four large canvasses. The painting on the far wall catches my attention first. It's stunning. A woman dressed in nothing but a man's white dress shirt. She's stretched out on a couch, one hand gripping the cushion, the other tucked between her slightly parted legs. Her head is tilted back, her mouth half open, eyes closed, sheer ecstasy shaping her features.

I'd know the shape of that body anywhere. I would recognize her from the pleasure on her face.

Beside me, I hear a small cry and I turn to see Maggie biting her lip, eyes fixed on the painting labeled DISCOVERY.

Her hand covers her mouth as her eyes scan the other portraits.

"I'll get everyone out," I whisper. "We'll close the room back up. It's not worth it."

She shakes her head, eyes brimming with tears. "No. I'm not hiding anymore. Let it be."

I feel completely helpless as I watch her look at the paintings, one by one, as if she's forcing herself to take in every detail, to catalogue her own sins.

"Holy shit," someone says behind us. I think it's Lizzy, but I don't turn to see.

A painting labeled FRIDAY MORNING shows a bed with a fluffy white comforter, a red head peaking out the top, eyes sleepy and seductive.

Another appears to place the viewer from the most erotic position between her legs. The perspective shows her inner thighs and bare stomach, her red hair covering her breasts.

Yet another appears to have been painted from the perspective of the person she's straddling. A yellow sundress is bunched around her hips, and her head is tilted to the side, her eyes closed, mouth parted in ecstasy.

Maggie spins a slow circle, taking in each painting, blood draining from her face.

By the time she looks at the last one, she's pale and unsteady. I hold her up.

"I'm fine." She steps back. "Fine."

She's not fine and we both know it, but she doesn't want to lean on me. Doesn't want to need me. Not anymore.

"I need to go." She turns on her heel and pushes through the crowd.

Maggie

Several smokers mingle on the front patio and eye me curiously as I exit the gallery. I excuse myself and follow the sidewalk away from the building to a garden area with the solitude I crave.

I should have never trusted Ethan. That is so obvious now I can only shake my head in bewilderment at the girl I was.

"I'm so sorry, Maggie."

I turn to see Will, regret written all over his expression, and my shoulders drop. Funny the difference a month makes. A month ago, I would have thought that exhibition was the worst thing that could have happened. Now, my heart is so torn up over Asher, the exhibit is only another bad bit of luck, but nothing life altering.

"I didn't know what was in there," Will says.

"It doesn't matter." Funny how it took me all these years and all this pain to realize that keeping a secret doesn't change the past. It doesn't correct our errors or mend the things we've broken.

The secret only harvests the hurt next to our hearts, blocking the sunlight from the spot where happiness is supposed to grow.

"I'm sorry about Asher," Will says. "He's not leaving her, then?"

I lift my eyes to his and shrug. "He says he is, but that isn't enough." My voice cracks and before I realize they're coming, tears are streaming down my face and my chest is shaking.

Will pulls me into his arms and strokes my hair as I struggle to breathe around choked sobs.

"I won't be that woman anymore."

Asher

I want to rage at someone, anyone. I want to tear these paintings off the walls and burn them.

"We didn't know," someone says behind me.

I spin around to see Will, hands tucked in his pockets, shoulders hunched.

My hands flex into fists and I step back away from the urge to take a swing.

When I got here, Maggie was outside crying. In Will's arms.

"I wouldn't have allowed it if I'd known," Will's saying as he eyes the paintings. "Not in my gallery. But Maggie asked me to leave them."

"Where is she?"

"She went to Brady's with her sisters," Will says, straightening. "You hurt her."

My jaw feels like it might snap it's so tight. I don't want to hear this from the man who just had the woman I love in his arms. But I can't deny it either.

He nods knowingly and slips out the door, leaving me alone to contemplate these paintings.

By the time I got done arguing with Juliana—explaining in no uncertain terms that our marriage is over—I had a long argument with myself about coming here tonight.

Maggie deserved to be pissed at me. With her history, I should have been more forthcoming about the state of my marriage. I'd be lying if I said it never occurred to me that the truth might hurt her, but I told myself it didn't matter because my marriage is nothing but a technicality at this point.

I need to go home and give her space. I need to get on my knees and pray like hell she'll come back to me.

But I have to do one more thing before I can leave.

chapter twenty-three

Maggie

I FINALLY fell asleep some time before dawn, but not before I cried. I cried for the lost young woman I'd become, the woman who'd trusted her shattered heart with a man and had lost it. I cried for the young woman who had placed her baby in a stranger's arms and said goodbye. I cried for my teenage self, the girl who had lost something precious to a man who hadn't been worthy and hadn't had permission.

I'd lain in bed, alone, remembering the only other time loneliness had struck me so deeply.

"Will you tell them that I want her name to be Grace?"

Sister Rose had frowned. *"Maggie, we talked about this. They can—"*

"Will you just tell them?"

Every week, pictures arrive in the mail with a short note.

Thank you for Grace. She is truly a blessing.

Would it be easier if all I'd known of the child I created had been those brief but precious moments in the hospital? Would it be easier if I didn't know my daughter has my red hair and freckles and her dad's dimples?

Would it be easier to sleep in my cold bed when I hadn't known the feel of a man who truly cared for me?

The only place I want to be is curled up on my mom's couch. Right now, I don't mind the doilies and cross-stitched pillows. I don't even mind the oversized golden crucifix that hangs above me.

The cushions shift beside me and I blink up at my mom.

"Here you go, sweetie," Mom says, handing me a steaming mug of tea.

"Thanks."

"Your sisters told me about Asher's wife."

I close my eyes. I can't look at her. Not now. I draw in a shaky breath. "I'm sorry." I shake my head. "I was trying to change."

"It's not your fault, sweetie."

I draw in a shaky breath. "Do you ever think that maybe dad was right about me?"

She gasps. "He wasn't." She shakes her head. "And I'm sorry I let him treat you like he did…after. We were both so heartbroken over what happened to our baby, and we handled it terribly. And I'm sorry for that."

"It wasn't your fault."

"The blame is more mine than yours, Margaret." Her face softens. "I have wished so many times to be able to change the past, to do right by you."

I can hardly breathe; my shattered heart is so painful against my lungs.

She studies me a long moment before nodding and pushing herself off the couch.

"Mom, wait."

My words stop my mother in her tracks. I haven't called her *Mom* since dad died. I never called her by her given name, either. She wouldn't have allowed that. I just haven't called her anything.

My throat is thick with emotion. "Thank you for letting me stay here."

"Of course," she says, her voice crackling on the edges with tears.

I study my tea. "Are you okay?"

She nods. "I like it when you call me 'Mom.' You haven't done that since you were fifteen."

"I…" I was a little shit who blamed her for things she couldn't control. Things that she would have given the world to save me from. Since there's no explaining, I hand her a fat envelope from my purse.

I can hardly breathe as she slides the pictures into her hand. And, as it always does, my heart breaks at the sight of my baby girl with her bright green eyes and wild red curls. Her mother sends me pictures every week. Pictures and gratitude expressed in stories about bath time, bottles, and cooing. I savor the packages like fine chocolate, and they tear me to shreds like razor blades.

I wait for my mother to get angry. For my lying. For my deception. I wait for that moment when she will finally be done with me. I wait but nothing happens. She flips through the pictures slowly, smiling and grimacing alternately, as if—maybe—she's imagining what seeing the pictures must be like for me.

When she makes it through the stack and returns her eyes to mine, she doesn't speak.

"They named her Grace," I say softly, my hands shaking as I take the pictures back.

Tears shimmer in her eyes. I haven't seen my mother cry since my father's funeral.

"I was pregnant when Will and I got engaged," I tell her. "I was pregnant with Ethan Bauer's baby." As the words slip from my mouth, they don't hurt like I expect them to. Instead, the truth is a salve to my abraded heart. "I was going to pretend it was Will's, and I couldn't. I couldn't do that to him. I couldn't do that to her. So I gave her up."

She settles back onto the couch and strokes my cheek. I don't realize I'm crying until I feel her wiping away my tears. I've cried enough in the last twenty-four hours to make up for years of dry eyes.

"I...suspected," my mother whispers. "I didn't know how to help you. I didn't know what you wanted. I should have..." My mom squeezes her eyes shut and shakes away the thought.

"I still hadn't forgiven myself for what happened in high school, and I—"

Mom's breath draws in sharply. "Baby," she whispers.

"I hated letting her go, but I was too ashamed to have a married man's baby. I didn't think I could ever face you again." I squeeze her hand. "I handled it in the only way I knew how."

"I think, Margaret Marie, that you handled it beautifully. And I am proud to have you as my daughter."

My mom wraps her thin arms around me, and I sink into the old, familiar warmth. I can't remember the last time I let my mother hug me, but it feels like returning home. She rocks me gently side to side and kisses my hair.

"What an amazing gift," she says simply, and the words tear me open. I cry into her chest.

When she pulls away, her eyes are wet and there are tears streaming down her face. "I've made a mess of my makeup," she mutters, but her smile says she doesn't really care.

Her hand feels frail in mine. "I'm going to take a walk down to the river."

She nods. "Have you called him?"

I look at the floor and shake my head. No need to say who *he* is. "I'm not ready yet."

"No!" Lizzy shouts. "No regrets about sleeping with Sexy Beast. Absolutely not."

I can't help but smile. She's so flipping cute. "He's married," I repeat softly.

Hanna's scanning through something on her phone, and when she hands it over to me, triumph gleams in her eyes.

She has some sort of gossip site pulled up and her phone is displaying the headline "Infinite Gray Hottie and Actress Wife On the Outs." I scroll through it to see a vague reporting of nothing but a rehashing of the title and a speculation that the couple has separated since the birth of their daughter.

"That was published two *years* ago, Mags," Hanna says.

I roll my shoulders back. "It doesn't matter. I won't be the other woman anymore."

The girls exchange a look, frowning.

"It just feels like Asher's getting a bum rap because of jerks from your past," Lizzy says.

Hanna nods. "Is that really fair?"

I shrug, pushing myself out of my chair. "If he wants to be with me, he can get a divorce."

"I guess," Hanna says softly.

"I'm going to step out for some fresh air," I say.

The girls nod. "We'll be there in a minute."

I'm halfway to the door when Will stops me.

"How you holding up?" he asks.

"I'm okay." And it's true. It's been a week since I walked in on Juliana naked in Asher's bed, and even though my heart aches with missing him, I'm more okay than I have been in years. Ironically, it's all thanks to him.

"I know this handsome blond guy who'd love to take you out sometime...when you're ready." Will gives a self-deprecating grin.

"I appreciate that," I say softly. "But you deserve more than to be my consolation prize."

"I would have settled for that."

I lift onto my tiptoes and press a kiss to his cheek. "And I love you for that."

chapter twenty-four

Asher

SHE CAME *back*.

It's all I can think. I'm consumed by it.

I sent her a text before I boarded my plane in New York tonight.

It's done.

That was all I wrote. Because I didn't know if the end of my marriage meant the beginning of something new with Maggie or if I'd lost my chance for that.

I came home to a dining room table covered in rocks, scraps, and shards of ceramic and glass.

What did she call this stuff? Tesserae?

There are little piles of it all over the table with note cards labeling each one.

A pile of glass shards, *Crystal serving platter from bridal shower.* A pile of sand, *From the bottom of the river.* Some slivers that glint in the light, *The Infinite Gray album.* A little gravel, *From the parking lot at Cajun Jack's.* Yellow and green chunks of plastic, *Baby bottles I never got to use.* There's even a tiny pile of old guitar picks and one final note.

I think we can make something beautiful with all this. Find me.

Maggie

I peel off my shirt and jeans then drop my bra and underwear to the ground and dive nude into the warm water.

I don't like to think what might have happened if Asher hadn't shown up at Brady's that night. I don't like to think what might have happened if he hadn't shown up in my life.

After I left the courthouse last week, I drove to Asher's house, but he wasn't here. I'd sent him a single text.

The text simply read: *Thank you for finding me.*

It wasn't long after that I found out he left town. I assumed he headed to New York to see his daughter. I couldn't blame him.

Then tonight, I got a text from him: *It's done.*

I can only hope that means what I think it does. I am only here because I think it means his marriage is over in every sense of the word now.

I turn through several laps, and I'm not surprised when I see him. I stop swimming and pull myself to the edge of the pool.

"Training for the Olympics?" He's wearing dark blue jeans, but his chest and feet are bare and my mouth goes dry at the expanse of his chest, at the V of muscle that dips into his jeans.

I swallow hard, remembering our first encounter here. "Sneak up on many girls?"

"Only the special ones." His eyes are hot, burning with something more than lust.

When he extends a hand, I take it and let him help me from the water. Then I stand there dripping in the moonlight as he runs his eyes over me.

My nipples harden in the cool air. Without speaking, he dips his head and licks a bead of water off one. My lungs empty, no room for air as the potent tonic of pleasure and love shoots into my veins. It starts cool and runs hotter until it settles between my legs. His big hands settle at my hips, the calluses of his fingertips curling into my ass as he takes my breast into his mouth. My breasts have always been about my lover's pleasure. They're large and awkward but men love them. But when Asher takes my breast into his hot mouth, when he scrapes his teeth across my nipple, when he sucks, I am lost in it. In him. I want him to keep doing this, to keep making me feel this way. I feel my control fracturing under the pressure, but I don't stop him because—for him—I'll let myself break.

I reach for him and unbutton his jeans. I push his pants and underwear from his hips. In a single motion, I drop to my knees and slide them down his legs.

His cock jumps, a breath from my lips, and my heart pounds at the sight of him, the memory of him.

"Stand up, Maggie." His voice is hard, thick with a need I understand.

In the chilly air, my skin breaks out in goose bumps.

Taking both of my hands in one of his big ones, Asher kicks his jeans away and leads me up the steps to his hot tub. I follow him, sinking into the hot, bubbling water.

He cups my face in his hands and stares down at me with those wild blue eyes. I wait for him to drop his lips to mine, but he doesn't.

"If I would have believed a miracle like you could come into my life, I would have ended my marriage last year. I would have been waiting and ready."

I touch his face, his stubble abrading my fingertips. I love this man so much my heart aches with it.

"You're trembling," he whispers against my ear.

I pull back so he can see me shake my head. I'm afraid to talk, afraid to speak the words lodged in my throat. Afraid I might lose it.

He holds me, and I cling to him like I've never clung to anyone. "I found you, sweetheart. You don't need to hold together anymore. I found you."

epilogue

Maggie
Eight Months Later

CAMPUS IS insane with the buzz about tonight's concert. Sinclair students stood in line for days waiting for tickets to Asher Logan's concert—his first by himself, and a kickoff to his fifty-campus tour for his new solo album *Unbreak Me*.

The auditorium is packed, and as the lights go down the crowd explodes in cheers.

The soft spotlights on the stage grow brighter as Asher steps out with his guitar, a fist raised in the air.

The wild shrieks of the girls in the front row fade into the background as I look at him, my heart pounding with pride, my stomach fluttering with nerves.

"Sinclair University, how are you tonight?" he shouts.

They respond with more noise, escalating until the room pulses at the edges with sheer volume and energy.

"Thank you for coming."

As if on cue, the roars quiet as they wait for him to begin.

"This first one's for my girl, Maggie." He turns to where I stand at the side of the stage and winks at me before returning his attention to the crowd. "It's called 'Unbreak Me.'"

The audience roars in appreciation.

He plays the opening chords of the song he wrote for me, and as he begins to sing, hot tears streak down my cheeks. I close my eyes and mouth the words.

I was nothing but a failure. A fucked-up, broken shame.
I was nothing but this emptiness. A shell ruined by fame.
Don't be afraid to shatter, baby, if that will set you free.
I'll find you in the pieces and that will unbreak me.

When he reaches the end of the song and the crowd's applause dies down, he turns to me again. "I love you, gorgeous."

"I love you too!" I shout back over the audience's screams.

I don't know if he hears me, but he grins, and my chest is so full of love, I might shatter, and I'm okay with that because I know he'll find me. Again and again.

The End

other titles by
Lexi Ryan

New Hope Series
Unbreak Me
Wish I May

Hot Contemporary Romance
Text Appeal
Accidental Sex Goddess

Stiletto Girls Novels
Stilettos, Inc.
Flirting with Fate

Decadence Creek Stories and Novellas
Just One Night
Just the Way You Are

contact

I love hearing from readers, so find me on my facebook page: facebook.com/lexiryanauthor, follow me on Twitter @writerlexiryan, shoot me an email at writerlexiryan@gmail.com, or find me on my website: www.lexiryan.com.

acknowledgements

As always, I owe the bulk of my gratitude to my husband and children. Brian, thank you for playing single dad while I wrapped up this book, but, more than that, thank you for believing in my dreams. With you holding my hand, it doesn't feel like a leap of faith but just another step. To my children, thank you for enjoying PB&J and frozen pizzas and understanding when Mommy needs to work. I love you all more than you'll ever know.

To the fabulous Nina, aka Violet Duke, thank you for believing in this book before I'd even committed to writing it. You saw it for what it could be and helped kick my butt until it became what it is today. You have mad skills, lady.

To everyone else who provided me feedback on and cheers for Maggie's story along the way—especially Marilyn Brant, Adrienne Hogan, Michael Miller, Megan Mulry, and Annie Swanberg—you're all awesome.

Many people helped with the research for this book. A huge thanks to Jim Archer for answering my many questions about the criminal justice system. Thanks to my artist brother Aaron for answering my questions about the art world and to my nurse sister Kim for explaining some ER protocol. Their answers were instrumental to my story. Any errors are my own.

Thank you to the team that helped me package this book and promote it. Sarah Hansen at Okay Creations designed my cover, and it truly takes my breath away. Arran at Editing720, thank you for the fast and thorough edits. Thanks to Giselle at Xpresso Book Tours for organizing the fantastic cover reveal and release day blitz, and to Julie at AToMR for organizing my reviews. You all earn every cent and more.

To all my writer friends on Twitter, Facebook, and my various writer loops, thank you for your support and inspiration. Lauren Blakely, thank you for featuring *Unbreak Me* in the back of *Trophy Husband*. Thanks to Violet Duke and Lisa Renee Jones for agreeing to share excerpts of their upcoming releases with my readers.

And last but certainly not least, thank you to my fans. I appreciate each and every one of you. I couldn't do this without you and wouldn't want to. Thank you for buying my books and telling your friends about them. Thank you for asking me to write more. You're the best!

play list

Unbreak Me Playlist

Ani DiFranco—*32 Flavors*
Nine Inch Nails—*Perfect Drug*
P!nk—*Slut Like You*
Cold Play—*Fix You*
The Fray—*How to Save a Life*
P!nk, featuring Nate Ruess—*Just Give Me a Reason*
Muse—*Madness*
Nine Inch Nails—*Hurt*
Ani DiFranco—*Gratitude*
Labrinth featuring Emeli Sandé—*Beneath Your Beautiful*
Rihanna featuring Mikki Ekko—*Stay*
Ani DiFranco—*Amazing Grace*
Josh Radin—*When You Find Me*

Sneak Peek of Escaping Reality by Lisa Renee Jones and Falling for the Good Guy by Violet Duke

Dear Readers: One of the few activities I love as much as writing is reading. On the following pages, you will find the description of and excerpts from two books I'm looking forward to. Though strikingly different in tone and subject matter, they both promise to be great, sexy reads: Lisa Renee Jones' *Escaping Reality* and Violet Duke's *Falling for the Good Guy*, both coming summer 2013. Enjoy!

Escaping Reality by Lisa Renee Jones
About the Book

He is rich, famous, and secretive and he will become her passion, her desire, her escape from a dark reality she so desperately craves…

At the young age of eighteen, tragedy and a dark secret force Lara to flee all she has known and loves to start a new life. Now years later, with a new identity as Amy, she's finally dared to believe she is forgotten–even if she cannot forget. But just when she lets down her guard down, the ghost's of her past are quick to punish her, forcing her back on the run.

On a plane, struggling to face the devastation of losing everything again and starting over, Amy meets Liam Stone, a darkly entrancing recluse billionaire, who is also a brilliant, and famous, prodigy architect. A man who knows what he wants and goes after it. And what he wants is Amy. Refusing to take "no" as an answer, he sweeps her into a passionate affair, pushing her to her erotic limits. He wants to possess her. He makes her want to be possessed. Liam demands everything from her, accepting nothing less. But what if she is too devastated by tragedy to know when he wants more than she should give? And what if there is more to Liam than meets the eyes?

Excerpt © Lisa Renee Jones
Chapter One

Amy…

My name is all that is written on the plain white envelope taped to the mirror.

I step out of the stall inside the bathroom of Manhattan's Metropolitan Museum, and the laughter and joy of the evening's charity event I've been enjoying fades away. Fear and dread slam into me, shooting adrenaline through my body. No. No. No. This cannot be happening and yet it is. It is, and I know what it means. Suddenly, the room begins to shift and everything goes gray. I fight the flashback I haven't had in years, but I am already right there in it, in the middle of a nightmare. The scent of smoke burns my nose. The sound of blistering screams shreds my nerves. There is pain and heartache, and the loss of all I once had and will never know again. Fighting a certain meltdown, I swallow hard and shove away the gut-wrenching memories. I can't let this happen. Not here, not in a public place. Not when I'm quite certain danger is knocking on my door.

On wobbly knees and four-inch black strappy heels that had made me feel sexy only minutes before and clumsy now, I step forward and press my palms to the counter. I can't seem to make myself reach for the envelope and my gaze goes to my image in the mirror, to my long white-blond hair I've worn draped around my shoulders tonight rather than tied at my nape, and done so as a proud reflection of the heritage of my Swedish mother I'm tired of denying. Gone too are the dark-rimmed glasses I've often used to hide the pale blue eyes both of my parents had shared, making it too easy for me to see the empty shell of a person I've become. If this is what I am at twenty-four years old, what I will be like at thirty-four?

Voices sound outside the doorway and I yank the envelope from the mirror and rush into the stall, sealing myself inside. Still chatting, two females enter the bathroom, and I tune out their gossip about some man they'd admired at the party. I suddenly need to confirm my fate. Leaning against the wall, I open the sealed envelope to remove a plain white note card and a key drops to the floor that looks like it goes to a locker. Cursing my shaking hand, I bend down and scoop it up. For a moment, I can't seem to stand up. I want to be strong. I have to be strong. I shove to my feet and blink away the burning sensation in my eyes to read the few short sentences typed on the card.

I've found you and so can they. Go to JFK Airport directly. Do not go home. Do not linger. Locker 111 will have everything you need.

My heart thunders in my chest as I take in the signature that is nothing more than a triangle with some writing inside of it. It's the tattoo that had been worn on the arm of the stranger who I'd met only once before. He'd saved my life and helped me restart my life, and he'd made sure I knew that symbol meant that I am in danger and I have to run.

Escaping Reality…Available for preorder now. Available everywhere July 22nd.

Falling for the Good Guy by Violet Duke
About the Book

From the evil author who left you hanging off a cliff in RESISTING THE BAD BOY comes the second book in the NICE GIRL TO LOVE series: Abby & Brian's story...

Abby Bartlett is well aware that everyone thinks she's in love with her best friend Brian. He is, after all, the type of man a nice girl should be with—the polar opposite of the bad boy—the kind of guy who didn't let his wife's decade-long illness stop him from showering her with a lifetime of love every second until her dying day. Yes, Brian has been the yardstick against which Abby has measured all other men. But everyone's wrong; she couldn't possibly be in love with him.

Because she's never once allowed herself that option.

It's taken a while but Brian Sullivan has finally come to terms with being a widower at the age of thirty, surviving the woman he spent half his life loving, a third of it losing. Truth is though, he wouldn't have 'survived' any of it really had it not been for Abby—sweet, incredible Abby—the woman he's never once had to picture his life without, never realized he couldn't truly live without. Until now. Now that he's finally able to love her the way she deserves, the way he knows she wants to be loved...by his brother.

Who's giving him exactly one chance to speak now or forever hold his peace.

Excerpt © Violet Duke

"You know you can still keep waiting on him, right?" Brian gazed into her eyes softly. "No one would fault you for it if you did. What you and my brother had was pretty intense."
That was an understatement.
Still, she didn't even hesitate. "No. No more waiting. It's time."

"Yeah?"

She gave him the most determined look she could scrounge up. "Yep."

He studied her for a beat and then leaned in closer. Until she could see every fleck of green in his teal blue eyes. "Your turn."

Confused, she drew back to a more thinking-friendly distance. "What?"

"Your turn to talk. You were going to say something earlier."

"Oh, right." She shook her head to clear it. Geez, maybe she was drunk. "I was just going to say something similar, actually. That no one would fault you for missing your wife during the holidays. You don't always have to be so strong. Not around me, at least."

"And now it's my turn to reply in a similar fashion. It's time."

She tilted her head. "What do you mean?"

"Are you serious about wanting to get over Connor?"

Was it *that* hard to believe? "I've told you, a deadline is a deadline."

"So this is now officially one of your wishes that you want to make into your reality?"

Heartbreakingly, it was. "Yes."

"Then let me help."

The corner of her mouth lifted up. The man was forever trying to right the world for everyone he cared about. "And you're going to help how exactly?"

"By any means necessary." He stole back the precious brain-clearing space she'd gained. "Are you going to make my task easy and let me kiss you at midnight, Abby-Bee?"

Abby-Bee. He hadn't called her that since college. She smiled wistfully at the memories the nickname brought back…for about a second before the rest of what he'd just said registered.

She almost spewed out a mouthful of beer in his face.

After two quick blinks she swore she could hardly recognize the man sitting beside her. Where was her warm, cuddly bear of a best friend? How did this hunk of a man with the scalding hot gaze get in her house?

And what on earth was she going to do with him?

"Brian—"

"Before you try to laugh this off and convince yourself I'm kidding, let me be clear." He slid his hands through her hair and gently tipped her face up to his. "I want to kiss you at midnight, Abby." He touched his forehead to hers. "All you have to do is let me."

It took a while for her brain to register all that he was saying, even longer for her body to make heads and tails of what he was doing. She'd basically just entered a world where red was green and warm was suddenly un-freakin'-believably hot.

She pulled back.

But her eyes couldn't seem to stop staring at his lips. "You can't kiss me, Brian. At least not how you're suggesting." *Because I'm still hopelessly in love with your brother.* "We're friends."

"Best friends," he agreed.

"Exactly." Somehow, she didn't think she was winning this debate.

"Why can't I kiss my best friend?" he argued back at barely a whisper. "Because she's an incredible woman I respect, admire, love, and know better than anyone else in the world—the same way she knows me? Or because she's the woman I'd just as soon cut my own heart out for before ever seeing hurt in any way?" He slid a thumb along her lower lip. "Or is it because she's the woman who's scared she might actually want to kiss me as much as I want to kiss her?"

Holy swizzle sticks. She was *definitely* losing this debate.

Falling for the Good Guy...Coming Summer 2013

This paperback interior was designed and formatted by

www.emtippettsbookdesigns.blogspot.com

Artisan interiors for discerning authors and publishers.

Made in the USA
Lexington, KY
24 November 2017